THE BRIDE OF DEMISE

2

Keishi Ayasato

Illustration by murakaruki

T0017238

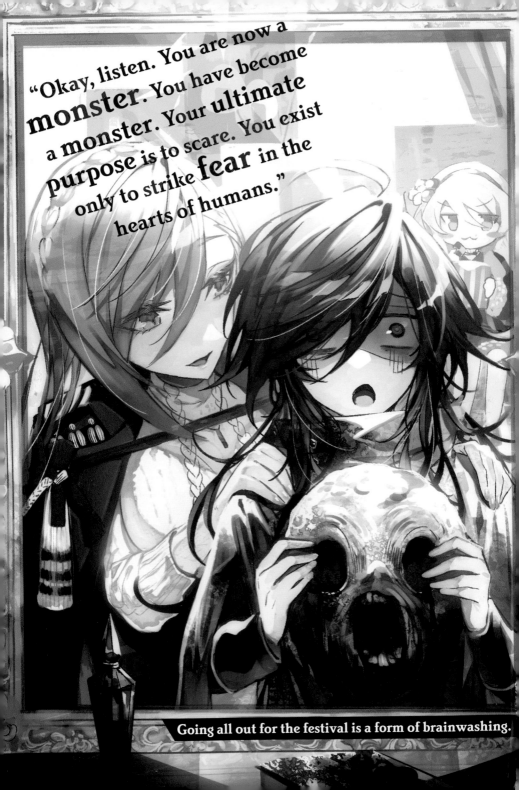

"Okay, listen. You are now a monster. You have become a monster. Your ultimate purpose is to scare. You exist only to strike fear in the hearts of humans."

Going all out for the festival is a form of brainwashing.

"The regular students have rejected us. There is nothing we can do about that. But I cannot allow those involved in this to live. We will get past this and then sink our teeth into their throats. ...Are you with me?!"

THE 3RIDE OF DEMISE

2

Keishi Ayasato

Illustration by
murakaruki

YEN ON

New York

THE BRIDE OF DEMISE

2

KEISHI AYASATO

Translation by Jordan Taylor
Cover art by murakaruki

This book is a work of fiction. Names, characters, places, and incidents are the product of the author's imagination or are used fictitiously. Any resemblance to actual events, locales, or persons, living or dead, is coincidental.

SHUEN NO HANAYOME Vol.2
©Keishi Ayasato 2020
First published in Japan in 2020 by KADOKAWA CORPORATION, Tokyo.
English translation rights arranged with KADOKAWA CORPORATION,
Tokyo through TUTTLE-MORI AGENCY, INC., Tokyo.
English translation © 2022 by Yen Press, LLC

Yen On
150 West 30th Street, 19th Floor
New York, NY 10001

Visit us at yenpress.com • facebook.com/yenpress • twitter.com/yenpress
yenpress.tumblr.com • instagram.com/yenpress

First Yen On Edition: November 2022
Edited by Yen On Editorial: Emma McClain, Rachel Mimms
Designed by Yen Press Design: Andy Swist

Yen On is an imprint of Yen Press, LLC.
The Yen On name and logo are trademarks of Yen Press, LLC.

The publisher is not responsible for websites (or their content) that are not owned by the publisher.

Library of Congress Cataloging-in-Publication Data
Names: Ayasato, Keishi, author. | Mura, Karuki, illustrator. | Taylor, Jordan (Translator), translator.
Title: The bride of demise / Keishi Ayasato ; illustration by murakaruki ; translation by Jordan Taylor.
Other titles: Shuen no hanayome. English
Description: New York, NY : Yen On, 2022.
Identifiers: LCCN 2022010509 | ISBN 9781975337940 (v. 1 ; trade paperback) |
ISBN 9781975337964 (v. 2 ; trade paperback) | ISBN 9781975338015 (v. 3 ; trade paperback)
Subjects: LCGFT: Fantasy fiction. | Light novels.
Classification: LCC PL867.5.Y36 S4813 2022 | DDC 895.63/6—dc23/eng/20220311
LC record available at https://lccn.loc.gov/2022010509

ISBNs: 978-1-9753-3796-4 (paperback)
978-1-9753-3800-8 (ebook)

10 9 8 7 6 5 4 3 2 1

LSC-C

Printed in the United States of America

The
Bride of
Demise

—

Table
of
Contents

Cover and illustrations by murakaruki

0. A SONG WITH NO NAME

This is a glimpse of a scene already over.
All part of the Gloaming now past.

Organs fell; blood flew.
Someone screamed, but it was quickly cut short.

Most of the opposing forces were fended off by the magic wall's defensive mechanisms and the most powerful teacher, Kagura, who stood atop it. But even that could not stop everything, for some enemies still slipped through.

That meant the Department of Combat, tasked with defending the interior of the Academy, witnessed hell.

None of the Special Types or Full Humanoids from deep within the ruins had reached the Academy yet, but many of the Type A kihei that had made it over the walls were far tougher than those normally encountered within the ruins.

By this point, none of the younger students were able to contribute to the battle. Those in their fourth year or above would surround a kihei and fire concentrated magic blasts at it. They might barely incapacitate it, or they might fail.

Several students lost their lives each time.

Students in Combat were always a mere few steps away from death—a fact they were well aware of. But none of them had anticipated seeing a hell like this unfold in front of their very eyes.

"I don't want to die… I don't want to die… I don't want to die!"

"Pull yourself together! Another one's coming!"

Another Type A leaped down from atop the magic wall. Its eight legs pierced the ground, sending tremors through the pavement. One insect-like leg mowed down a student, slicing through their magic armor, before flicking it off to the side, contents and all.

Guts splattered across the pavement.

The Combat students ignored this and let loose with machine-gun fire. As they did, another kihei appeared.

These enemies were tough, their attacks devastating.

The Department of Medicine made the rounds, providing aid to any survivors in need, but the majority of students were killed instantly.

"…So this is 'a sea of disaster and hell,' huh? So this is the Gloaming?" murmured one Combat student. Nonetheless, their squad had managed to bring down a number of kihei after considerable machine-gun fire. Using the superhuman strength of their magic armor, one fifth-year veteran drove a stake into a kihei's head.

With the kihei neutralized, they barked to those around them, "How many did we lose?"

"Three already… There's another one! Get in formation!"

This time, a snakelike kihei slithered down the magic wall.

Its body crushed one straggler, turning them into mincemeat.

"I wanna get out of here… I wanna get out of here… I wanna get out of here…!" muttered one of the first-years. But where would he go? This was the Academy, where students belonged.

The kihei swung its tail, sending another student flying. The trembling first-year saw it was his friend and rushed toward her. Her helmet was broken. Through the cracks, he could see her forehead, a portion peeled off, revealing the fleshy red substance underneath like the inside of a pomegranate. But she was still breathing.

She spoke, as if half in a dream: "Singing…"

"Don't talk; you'll make your injuries worse."

"I hear…singing."

"Singing?"

The first-year narrowed his eyes and focused his attention on the ambient noise. He couldn't hear anything except screams and shouts.

Even as his friend sank further toward death, she repeated those words.

"I hear…singing."

There were several other reports of similar occurrences.

A number of people on the edge of death during the Gloaming reported hearing an odd singing.

Kou Kaguro was powerful, which is why he wasn't able to learn this information.

The singing was beautiful.
It was lonely.
And it was sad.

In the end, the Department of Combat lost 20 percent of its students. Considering the hell they had faced, it was a miraculously low number.

And yet that first-year couldn't forget the song his friend had spoken of before she died.

It was almost as if someone far, far away, was singing an invitation to death.

The Bride of Demise

PROLOGUE

Kou Kaguro opened his violet eyes.

He looked down at his chest.

The hilt of a knife protruded from his uniform. Blood dripped slowly from the end.

With each beat of his heart, the hilt twitched up and down. The blood running along its length looked terribly vivid. The long blade was embedded completely in his chest.

Intense pain struck him, and he knew.

He'd been stabbed.

He slowly looked up and asked the person in front of him: "…Why?"

There was no response. She just smiled vaguely back at him.

He had never imagined she might kill him. He thought they'd had a good relationship. But at the same time, he thought:

It makes sense she would kill me.

During his fifteen thousand repetitions, she was the one he had treated most cruelly. But there was no way she could know that. He had no idea what had motivated this act of violence.

But he didn't have time to think about that.

She grabbed the hilt of the knife, twisted it, then pulled the blade from his chest.

It gouged a hole in his guts. Blood spilled to the ground.

His vision wavered from the shock.

The scenery of the Academy around him shook and swam.

His body leaned forward, and he collapsed.

The very last image to surface in his mind was that of two beautiful figures, one white, one black. He recalled the smiles of his Brides and clung to the memory.

He was dying.

In that moment, he concentrated and closed his eyes.

And he traveled back in time, to before he was killed.

Kou Kaguro opened his violet eyes.

He was surrounded by a heavy, almost viscous darkness.

He cocked his head. It looked like he hadn't jumped to the place he'd intended.

Everything around him was filled with that swirling blackness, except for a single point. There was one spot that shone with a pale-blue light. Unfamiliar inorganic walls curved up into the darkness.

The light emanated from something strange.

A pair of organic wings that looked ready to fall apart.

The wings resembled an owl's and pulsated with blue light. They were deformed. Between the stiff-looking feathers ran countless veinlike cables.

The wings were spread wide on each side. They weren't mounted on the wall, but they were perfectly still, not moving in the slightest.

Kou slowly turned his gaze.

His eyes slid down the smooth curve of the wings to where they attached.

In between them stood a girl, the wings growing out of her back.

Her white skin was like a corpse's, her purple hair like a finely crafted wig.

"…Who are you?" asked Kou.

The girl didn't reply.

Without a word, she opened her eyes.

Those misty eyes stared at Kou. He was relieved; she seemed able to understand him. But the next moment, her lips curled oddly. Her mouth opened, and shrill laughter poured out.

The sound reverberated, dreadfully sinister, just like the bell that marked the arrival of the Gloaming.

1. THE SUDDEN TRANSFER STUDENT

"Heyooo… You awake?"

Kou Kaguro opened his violet eyes.

He saw someone's face, with a classroom in the background.

The person, who Kou knew well, was peering back at him.

He had white hair, one blue and one black eye. His bangs were long, and the rest of his hair was cut roughly.

Kou looked the man up and down.

Deep scars stood prominently on his face and neck. His heavily decorated military uniform was covered with a worn, shabby coat. Kou was already quite familiar with it.

Kou belonged to class one hundred in the magic Academy, a class that was kept hidden—a class that "did not exist."

The most powerful squadron: Pandemonium.

And this man, Kagura, was their teacher.

His wasn't a face Kou wanted to see right after waking up, much less when he'd just had a nightmare. Kou pressed his hand to his abdomen over the lingering phantom pain as he shook his head.

"I'm awake… At least, now I am."

"You look awful. Did you have a bad dream?" asked Kagura casually. His intuition was sharp.

Kou frowned and pursed his lips. He had the feeling that if he answered poorly, this conversation could run long. But ultimately, it didn't matter whether Kou responded.

Carelessly, Kagura made the worst possible guess. "Was it a precognitive dream?"

"I was stabbed in the stomach… And then I was in the dark. I wonder where it was… And then I met some strange girl. You think that could be in my future?"

"Aaah. That kind of dream. It's not impossible." He meaninglessly twirled his fingers, then smiled flippantly. "I mean, I'd expect you to catch some glimpses of unfamiliar memories due to the influence of Millennium Black Princess. And now you have the power to go back in time… That could have any number of side effects."

Midway through, Kagura's tone had switched from joking to serious.

Kou grimaced.

Did that mean he would eventually experience the events of his dream?

He pressed his hand against his stomach where he was stabbed.

He felt pain lingering there, still vivid. The skin hadn't yet stopped its light convulsions, and as he checked it, he suddenly realized he'd forgotten a very important piece of information.

Wait… Who stabbed me?

"Koooooooooooou!"

"Hey, White Princess. Don't sprint through the… Ah, she's not listening," said Kagura.

Just as Kou was falling deep into thought, a white mass came flying at him. It crashed into him with such force that he was nearly knocked backward. But a pair of slender arms grabbed him and held him fast. The girl drew Kou into her chest and hugged him close.

"Are you awake?" she chirped. "I've been waiting for you to wake up. Let's have lunch outside!"

Her innocent eyes gleamed, and she grinned from ear to ear.

Her blue eyes were like the sky, her white hair like the snow.

Her arms and legs were graceful, and the slender yet tempered build of her body brought to mind a steel sword.

This was White Princess, Kou Kaguro's Bride.

Although Kagura was Kou's teacher, this conversation with his student was mere idle chatter. In other words, morning classes were already over. It seemed that White Princess had been resisting the urge to go outside as she waited for Kou to wake up. She bounced impatiently, as if she could barely contain herself.

She whispered what felt like a song of praise to their carefree everyday routine. "Hee-hee, I'm so happy to hold you like this."

"I'm happy, too, but...White Princess, my neck kind of hurts," said Kou.

He'd suffered a fair bit of damage when she slammed into him. He rubbed his aching neck, but he was smiling nonetheless.

Just then, an exasperated voice came from farther back in the classroom.

"White Princess, if you hug him with all your might, things could end in disaster. It's perfectly fine for a Bride to treasure their Groom, but you should show a bit more self-restraint."

"You're being ridiculous, Hikami. There's no holding restraining a young lady's feelings."

"...This happens all the time anyway. He must be used to it by now."

"If Kou was sent flying by that, it just means he needs more training. The weak are the first to die."

Kou looked up. The four of them must have been waiting on Kou just like White Princess. He saw their familiar faces at the top of the stairs that led up to the back of the classroom.

The red-haired boy with an eye patch was Ryuu Hikami. The girl with chestnut-colored hair and gentle, drooping eyes was Mirei Tachibana. The boy with androgynous features and a scarf covering his mouth was Rui Yaguruma. And the incredibly petite girl with blond hair was Tsubaki Kagerou.

Kou waved back at them.

As he did, White Princess rubbed her cheek against him and practically purred like a kitten. She really did seem happy. He stroked her silvery-white hair and glanced around the classroom.

It was filled with warm and pleasant chatter.

Kou took some time to reflect.

It's a miracle everyone's here, together again.

The events of the other day...

To Kou, their repetitions filled a vast expanse of time. He turned his thoughts back to the past.

* * *

History can be divided into two major periods:

Before the kihei appeared and after.

The word *kihei* could be written with the characters for *demon* and *soldier*. Or it could be written with the characters for *machine* and *soldier*. Either one was fine.

All they did was attack humans. They didn't eat humans; they just killed them.

Put simply, they were humanity's enemy.

Before Erosion… Imperial Year 25 BE.

The kihei abruptly appeared and attacked the empire, throwing humanity into chaos. Countless kihei invaded imperial territory. Contact with other countries was cut off, leaving the empire isolated. Ever since, they had been forced to fight a long and grueling war on their own.

Those "other countries" that used to exist had long ago faded from memory. The empire's independent magic research allowed the country to build impenetrable defenses.

This academy was also part of those plans.

Large numbers of pupils gathered in these houses of learning.

All of them, including Kou Kaguro, were official students.

Not just students but soldiers, too. They studied and also served as the empire's infantry.

The students existed for the purpose of fighting the kihei.

However, a fraction of the kihei were found to require a human master. Once they had encountered a worthy partner, they would request a contract. Those kihei tended to perceive this contract as a marriage and viewed their partner as their spouse. Eventually, these contracts came to be called marriage, with the kihei and human involved referred to as the Bride and Groom, respectively.

Pandemonium, then, was a class comprised entirely of students married to kihei Brides.

Kou had once nearly died deep within the ruins. There he encountered a kihei belonging to the Princess Series, the most powerful type of kihei. She was the previously unconfirmed seventh member of the series, and her alias was Curtain Call. That kihei was White Princess. She had saved him and entered a contract with him.

Afterward, Kou was welcomed into Pandemonium.

Things were peaceful for a while. But then the Academy was struck by the worst possible disaster.

When faced with that *one exception*, it was the students' duty to serve as a shield, defending their country to the death.

That *one exception*—the Gloaming.

When it occurred, the kihei all rushed at humans in a coordinated blood frenzy. They left the ruins, moving far beyond their usual range of activity, and attacked the closest location with large numbers of humans.

In other words, the Academy.

Perhaps the single most important reason for establishing this school of magic, the Twilight Academy, was to prevent such invasions.

During the Gloaming, a terrible, tragic battle unfolded, leading to the deaths of everyone in Pandemonium.

But by consuming White Princess, Kou gained a portion of her functions. He used that ability to travel back in time. After repeating the past fifteen thousand times, he finally succeeded in suppressing the source of the Gloaming.

And so Kou and all his friends returned alive.

Furthermore, concerning the events of the Gloaming, there was one other person who must not be forgotten.

The girl who traveled back in time before Kou, soaring to the past on mechanical wings. The one who went back to become the queen of the kihei, to be defeated by Pandemonium and change history: the other White Princess.

Millennium Black Princess.

She was currently in the ruins outside the Academy. Kou had managed to keep everyone alive, including her. That was the prize he had earned from his relentless repetitions.

Of all his friends, only White Princess knew of this.

All of them were here now.

That in itself was nothing less than a miracle.

* * *

Of course, that didn't mean there were no losses.

Student casualties comprised 20 percent of Combat students and less than 10 percent of regular students.

Pandemonium lost one member from the Wasp Rank and two members from the Flower Rank.

The dead wouldn't return, but that was the lowest casualty rate in the Academy's history.

Once the students had cast off their despair, the school buildings erupted in a whirlwind of excitement.

Services for the dead had concluded just the other day, and now there was talk of holding a festival to commemorate overcoming the Gloaming. Kou didn't have any details, though.

Pandemonium doesn't officially exist as a class. We probably won't be involved in the festival at all, he thought.

"Kou!" A voice interrupted his wandering thoughts. White Princess tugged his arm and cried, "Kou, hurry! Hikami's sandwiches are waiting for us!"

"That sounds wonderful; let's g—"

"All right, okay. I know you're all excited about your thrilling lunches, but just hold on a minute!" Kagura said just as Kou was responding to White Princess. Kagura lightly clapped his hands together and circled around the lectern to block Kou and White Princess's path.

Normally, Kagura left the classroom the moment class ended, so this was a rare occurrence. Kou's face stiffened. He wondered if Pandemonium had received a request.

Other students had been about to leave the classroom, too. Kagura called out to each one in turn, stopping them. "Okay, stop! Don't pretend you didn't hear me! Wait, I said!"

"No way."

"It's lunchtime."

"Try again later."

"Seriously, guys, come on!"

This started up their regular routine. Kagura pouted. Then students taunted him, telling him to knock it off because it wasn't cute. He jumped, fluttering the hem of his coat. But then he froze completely.

With a seemingly serious expression, he stepped forward and said, "Fine, out of my way. I'll just go get her. She's in the waiting room anyway."

Kagura left the classroom for a moment. His students might treat him casually, but he was still the most powerful teacher. And there was always the chance that he had some orders for them. No student dared slip out in

his absence. Though rowdy, the members of Pandemonium waited obedi-
ently for Kagura's return.

He was back less than a minute later.

"Sorry for the wait," he said. "Your teacher has returned!"

No one responded, but everyone narrowed their eyes.

Behind Kagura was a female student. She was wearing a slightly mod-
ified version of the standard crimson-and-black military-style uniform.
Her long skirt was adorned with classical frills. Her skin was pale white,
set off attractively by her lustrous black hair. She was gazing down at the
floor, making it hard to see her face, but her posture and overall impression were enough that anyone could tell she was quite the beauty.

All the students were on edge, wondering who she was and what was
going on.

In a grand voice, Kagura gave an announcement.

"All right, let me introduce you to the new transfer student."

The girl lifted her head. Kou immediately swallowed a yelp.

Every member of Pandemonium opened their eyes wide.

The air in the classroom grew thick with tension and hostility.

But Kagura paid none of that any mind as he continued:

"Her name is Millennium Black Princess."

This was the queen of the kihei; she was supposed to be in the ruins.

But now, Millennium Black Princess was standing in front of Kou and
his classmates.

* * *

"Seriously?"

"This is crazy."

"She must be trying to pick a fight."

"Wait, there might be some explanation."

The students' reactions were surprisingly calm. Everyone seemed to have their emotions under control, all things considered.

Kou, on the other hand, was flung into a swirling vortex of confusion.

Only he and White Princess, who he'd told, knew that Millennium Black Princess was actually the other White Princess. And now, with that fierce battle behind them, she was also Kou's second Bride.

Kou, of course, had felt bad about leaving her alone in the ruins outside the Academy, but he'd never expected to see her suddenly standing in the classroom, wearing a school uniform.

He simply couldn't understand how this had happened. It felt absurd.

What the hell is going on here? he thought, but he didn't have time to be confused.

A slashing strike was heading straight for Black Princess.

"Hmph."

"Ah!"

There was a harsh clash of metal.

It was Sasanoe's sword. Kou had blocked the fatal strike with one of White Princess's feathers.

Sasanoe wore a crow mask and was a student of Phantom Rank, the most powerful rank in Pandemonium.

Until now, he had been standing near the edge of the classroom, staring at the ceiling in boredom. But then, without a sound, he had rapidly moved, drawn his sword, and attacked Black Princess.

Kou, too, had reacted soundlessly. In a flash, he had accepted one of White Princess's feathers and blocked Sasanoe's attack. If he hadn't improved his coordination with his Bride to the limit over those fifteen thousand repetitions, he wouldn't have been able to stop the attack. That's how fierce Sasanoe's strike was.

Sasanoe held his fluid blade fast. Kou kept their swords crossed.

"Sasanoe, please step back!" said Kou.

"She should have been prepared to die the moment she stepped into enemy territory," roared Sasanoe. "Why is she here if not to offer up her own head?!"

The others in Pandemonium nodded their agreement. Any student who stepped into the ruins understood they were risking death, regardless of their own relative power. They were resolved to walk directly into their own grave.

In that light, Millennium Black Princess's actions seemed careless.

Kou accepted that much was true, but even so, he raised his voice. "She's not our enemy anymore! In that case, can you accept her?"

"You're quite the optimist if you think words will change anything. Fool."

Sasanoe stared directly at Kou from behind the crow mask. Kou returned his gaze.

That was when Hikami raised his hands and frantically tried to stop them. "I—I don't know what the heck's going on, but that's enough! Calm down, you two!"

"Looks like Sasanoe decided to show up for once. What a surprise," whispered Tsubaki casually. Sasanoe ordinarily skipped classes. Apparently, Tsubaki was more alarmed by this than by the current situation.

Sasanoe quickly withdrew his sword. It was a simple feint, but the sheer simplicity of the trick that threw Kou off-balance. Sasanoe immediately stepped forward.

His blade traced a complicated trajectory as it headed for Millennium Black Princess.

But before it could connect, it was caught by someone's bare hands.

"What are you doing, Shirai?" Sasanoe asked in a low whisper.

"Hikami's right. I think you should calm down. Kou's a Phantom Rank, just like us. And I see him as a man worthy of some trust. Nameless feels the same. So then, isn't it our duty as upperclassmen to hear him out? Don't you agree, Yurie?"

In the blink of an eye, the well-built student named Shirai had stepped right up to them. His formless Bride, Nameless, coated his hands, allowing him to stop Sasanoe's sword. Nameless's edges twitched, as if trying to signal Kou.

Yet another voice responded to Shirai.

"Hee-hee, Sister doesn't seem to hate Kou, either. So ignoring him and cutting up Millennium Black Princess would make you a bad boy. Why don't you just calm down for a moment, Sasanoe, hmm?"

The voice belonged to Yurie, a female student with dreamy eyes and black hair. Behind her stood Sister, her Full Humanoid Bride, arms crossed. Supposedly, Sister usually had a more mechanical appearance, but she was currently wearing a dress that Yurie had made specially for her. With it on, she looked nearly human enough to be a Princess Series. She glanced at Kou and nodded slightly.

These two, along with Sasanoe and Kou, were the only four Phantom Rank students. Upon hearing the words of his fellows, Sasanoe frowned. Kou bowed his head to the two of them.

Unlike those of Shirai and Yurie, Sasanoe's Bride, Crimson Princess, wasn't present. He'd probably had her stay in their room through the tiresome classes. But her absence didn't matter. Shirai didn't seem willing to use his Bride for anything other than defense at the moment. Yurie was the same.

So long as the Brides weren't turned to offense, the situation was at an impasse.

Kagura frowned as he watched this unfold. Then he seemed to realize something. "Oh," he started, "did I say Millennium Black Princess? I meant to gloss over that part and just introduce her as Black Princess. Oops."

"That's not the problem! You can't hide her by changing her name! Why the hell is Millennium Black Princess, the queen of the kihei, in the Academy and wearing a uniform?" shouted Sasanoe.

"Yeah, exactly."

"When you say it out loud, it sounds totally crazy."

"Only Sasanoe could make it sound so convincing."

The students of Pandemonium were in agreement with Sasanoe.

The situation was getting even more out of hand.

The members of Pandemonium had seen Millennium Black Princess during the Gloaming. They weren't about to mistake the face of their enemy for someone else. After all, they had fought her to the death. And while their wounds may now be healed, they had each suffered injuries both big and small.

And yet that's all Kagura'd had to say about the situation?

Kou racked his brain, trying to make sense of it.

…Transfer student? Gloss over?

"What I'm trying to say is that this isn't the queen of the kihei," said Kagura without hesitation. "This is Black Princess. She's a new student who was sent to the Academy when her parents died. Her Bride is a Type A.

I invited her here." He puffed out his chest, unabashed. "That's all. The paperwork's already done. *There is no queen of the kihei.*"

At Kagura's words, Sasanoe's mouth twisted into a sarcastic frown. He understood what their teacher meant. Everyone did.

There's not much information on Millennium Black Princess, thought Kou.

The only people who had seen her up close for a prolonged time were the members of Pandemonium. With her wearing a school uniform, no one else would even realize she was a kihei.

That was why Kagura had introduced her, the queen of the kihei, to Pandemonium as a mere human.

Sasanoe put away his sword for a moment. He spoke in a clipped whisper, "Insufficient. Explain."

"Let me say something," offered Kou, not waiting for Kagura to speak. "It's difficult to explain in a way that you'll accept so…I'll get right to the point. She is not our enemy anymore. I, Kou Kaguro, guarantee it, on my life."

Kou walked to the top of the stairs and took Black Princess's hand. Her eyes, the same color as her hair, blinked, and she looked away.

He squeezed her hand tight, then continued. "The rampage that occurs during the Gloaming when the queen gathers magic is over. And before that, she had never killed a single student… Millennium Black Princess isn't hostile toward us anymore."

"He's right. I…I don't want to kill anyone. I don't want to hurt anyone, or make them cry, or make them sad, or make them suffer," said Black Princess, her voice trembling. She squeezed Kou's hand back and closed her eyes.

She trembled slightly, then deeply bowed her head.

"I have done such horrible things to you all. I don't expect you to believe me… But please…would you believe me?"

A white form suddenly appeared beside Black Princess. A girl had leaped up to stand shoulder to shoulder with her.

Kou looked at the girl in surprise.

It was White Princess, her blue eyes aglint. "I will also stake all of my organic components on it," she announced. "She is not our enemy."

"White Princess…," murmured Kou.

"What do you think, everyone? Will you believe us?" asked White Princess. It was an appeal with no proof to back it up.

Their explanation was severely lacking in any concrete basis for trust, but Kou and White Princess knew. The members of Pandemonium preferred "That's just the way it is" over anything legitimately convincing.

There were a few moments of silence, but sure enough, the responses that came back were lighthearted.

"A Phantom Rank Bride and Groom guaranteeing it? That's enough for me."

"We are Pandemonium. Our Brides and our skills are everything."

"I don't mind so long as she's useful."

The hostility quickly dissipated. Many of the students were welcoming in their own way.

Kou nodded in response and looked toward Hikami and the others. They looked back at him in confusion, so he mouthed, "I'll explain later." Neither Shirai nor Yurie seemed opposed, either. They nodded happily and returned to their seats. Next, Kou turned toward Sasanoe.

Behind the crow mask, he seemed to be thinking. Eventually, he let out a small snort and said, "There's no logic to that. You're a hopeless fool. But…no one did more during the Gloaming than you. Guess that gives you the right to do what you want, just this once."

"Thank you, Sasanoe."

"Don't thank me. Fool."

His vocabulary as lacking as usual, Sasanoe sheathed his sword. He'd apparently accepted the situation as well.

Kou let out a sigh of relief. He turned to face Black Princess once again and mouthed a question to her, asking why she was here.

She brought a hand to her bountiful bosom and whispered, "I'll explain everything later… Kou, I am so happy to be by your side."

She gave a gentle, clumsy smile. White Princess frowned.

These two had a complicated relationship.

Kou moved before the conversation could go on any longer. He descended the stairs, taking his Brides with him.

And so the uproar settled.

Millennium Black Princess's unexpected transfer was safely resolved.

That was the end of that. Or so everyone assumed, letting down their guard. But Kagura continued.

"Uuuuh, so there's actually something else we need to talk about. Wait a sec."

The students tensed. Kou felt his body go stiff as he wondered what else could possibly happen.

Then, with a very serious expression, Kagura said:

"We're gonna be contributing something to the festival commemorating the end of the Gloaming. Anyone want to be in charge?"

Every student present shot Kagura a look of exasperation.

He never bothered to read the room.

The abrupt change of subject was enough to give a person whiplash.

The Bride of Demise

2. BLACK PRINCESS'S REGRET

"Kagura suggested it."

Kou Kaguro was in his own room.

After class finished, he, White Princess, and Black Princess had headed there.

Pandemonium didn't have dorms. Instead, they used some of the guest rooms in Central Headquarters.

Black Princess was currently sitting on the overly opulent bed with her legs tucked under her.

She'd already gotten ready for bed. Her hair was down, and she'd switched her uniform out for a thin black gown. Her long black tresses cascaded over the white bedsheets.

Her back was perfectly straight as she sat, and she spoke almost in singsong.

"He said, 'No one will approve of Kou Kaguro having two Princess Series Brides, even more so if one of them is Millennium Black Princess. So why don't you hide the fact that you're a kihei and come to the Academy? ...He also said he could prepare all the necessary documents and forgeries."

"Mm, that teacher can do anything." Kou heaved a sigh from where he sat on the bed.

He imagined Kagura jumping and doing a silly victory pose.

Kou couldn't really claim Kagura was completely different from him.

The fact that this man was the closest existence to his own was a sore spot for Kou. But perhaps he should be grateful for Kagura's flexibility.

Kou didn't want Black Princess to be left in the ruins for who knew how long. He was so fortunate to have her here with him. Kou turned to face Black Princess. She smiled gently.

He spoke with unbridled joy. "I'm so glad you're by my side now, Black Princess."

"Me too, Kou. I was lonely for so long. Being with you is like witnessing a ray of sunshine pierce a world consumed by darkness. The first bright light in a hundred, a thousand, even ten thousand years."

"Black Princess…"

"Kou…"

"Hmph…"

"Did you hear a strange sound just now?" asked Kou as he looked to the side to see a monster at the end of the bed.

It wasn't a real monster, but White Princess's silvery-white head poking over the edge of the bed from where she sat on the floor.

Various emotions played out on her face as she, for some reason, chewed on the bedsheets.

"Come on, what's wrong, White Princess? Spit that out!"

"Kou already explained, and to be honest, I had sensed it… You are me. You are my own self. And so I understand your feelings. I can't stop you," said White Princess, her tone serious, affection in her eyes as she looked at Black Princess. But then she shook her beautiful head like she was lost. Her voluminous hair swayed from side to side. "But, but, but, but, but but… I don't know what to do about all these emotions inside me. I don't know how to deal with all this. I just can't…"

She crashed her forehead into the bed.

Kou got down from where he was sitting. He slipped his arms around White Princess's sides and lifted her. He patted her back, then set her on the edge of the bed.

As he gently patted her head, he told her, "White Princess, I love you. You don't have anything to be worried about."

"That's right, White Princess. I know where I, Black Princess, belong. I have no intention of stealing Kou from you. Just knowing he's still alive makes me happy enough to die."

"W-wait. That makes me sound like a bad person. I don't mean to say you can't be by his side. Ugh, this is so frustrating, I don't even know what to say. I'm weak," said White Princess with a frown. Black Princess's brow furrowed as she, too, wasn't certain what to do.

The two of them fell silent.

After White Princess gathered herself again, she patted Black Princess's head. Black Princess simply accepted the gesture.

The sight was enough to make Kou smile.

Now, then, thought Kou. He racked his brain, trying to decide how to deal with Black Princess.

Normally, she would have been subject to the first test after being transferred into Pandemonium—the battle test—but she'd been exempted. Everyone knew how powerful she was, after all. There was no point in measuring it now.

But Kou had heard that the second test would go ahead without any changes. That was the test to determine if a Groom could prevent their Bride from going on a rampage. During the test, the Bride entering Central Headquarters—Black Princess in this case—would be monitored for any abnormalities. They weren't supposed to watch while the people being surveilled were getting changed, so it was possible Kou and the two Princesses weren't being monitored at the moment. That time would soon come, though.

They had to be careful what they said from here on out.

Kou spoke to Black Princess, hoping she might go to sleep early.

"You must be tired today, Black Princess. Do you want to go to sleep now?"

"This means the three of us will be sharing a bed from now on, right?" asked Black Princess.

White Princess's mouth curved down in frustration; she looked troubled.

This upset Black Princess. She laced and unlaced her fingers, uncertain what to do.

After thinking long and hard, Black Princess tentatively ventured, "Actually, I don't deserve to be beside Kou. You said such nice things about me, but I really have hurt a lot of people. The darkness of the ruins really is the bed most suited for me. I should go back."

"Ah, no way, Black Princess! That is not happening!" cried White Princess, her voice almost a song. Black Princess blinked.

The expression on White Princess's face was no longer irritation. She reached out her arms and grabbed ahold of Black Princess, then pushed her back onto the bed.

Black and white hair mingled together and fell across the sheets. Surprised, Black Princess kicked her thin cloth-covered legs. White Princess kept her from escaping and looked down at her.

Her blue eyes gleamed as she said, "Do you think our Kou would let you go, when you are so worried? Do you think I would? I won't accept you drowning in darkness forever. You should live in the light."

"But I...have done so much harm."

"That may be true, Black Princess," said Kou gently. Black Princess jumped. Kou sat softly on the edge of the bed and reached out a hand to slowly and gently stroke her cheek. "But I know. I know that everything you accomplished was for me. If you're worried about your sins, then they're mine now. I'll bear them for you."

"And me too. You are me. And you are Kou's other Bride. Take pride in that," said White Princess.

"...You two..."

Black Princess's face twisted like a child's as heavy tears fell from her eyes.

She cried, completely vulnerable. Her shoulders hunched, and her slender body radiated the despair and loneliness she'd born for eternity. Kou and White Princess lay beside her on either side.

They hugged her.

With her hands over her face, she whispered, "Thank you, thank you so much... I was alone forever. It was so, so long..."

Her tears overflowed along with her words, falling like gemstones.

She sounded nearly heartbroken as she finally put her own wishes into words.

"I want to live. I want to live with the two of you."

"I want that, too, Black Princess," said Kou.

"Yes, let's live together, Black Princess," said White Princess.

Black Princess nodded firmly, over and over.

Eventually, she continued, her tone serious and her words slow. "...Do you think I can make it up to everyone in Pandemonium, too?"

"They're not the kind to dwell too much on that sort of thing," said Kou with a smile. In reality, no one in Pandemonium was the type to hold a grudge. Even against someone who had hurt them. They'd never say anything bad about someone they'd accepted as a companion. Kou was only worried about Sasanoe—and his pride as a warrior. But even he would come around eventually.

As Kou spoke for the others, Black Princess started crying again.

Eventually, her tears ran out, and her breathing slowed. White Princess closed her eyes as well, her arms wrapped around Black Princess's shoulders.

Kou stroked both their heads.

"Good night, you two. Sweet dreams."

He gently leaned over and gave each of his beloved Brides a quick kiss on the cheek.

* * *

The next day, the three of them had finished changing into their uniforms when there came a knock on the door.

Kou stood. Black Princess looked uneasy. He then attempted to reassure her: "It's probably Hikami and the others."

Yesterday, Kou had shot them a look saying he would explain everything later, but he still hadn't done so.

He quickly walked over to the door, opened it, and found himself face-to-face with a massive amount of luggage. His eyes grew wide. Examining the stack, he saw cloth of every color, a mountain of thread, the tilted lids of boxes, and all sorts of other containers.

"What is this?" Kou asked, surprised.

"We're coming in, Kou," said Tsubaki, several boxes stacked atop her head.

"The classroom's in chaos. We brought everything we might need to make sure it doesn't disappear somewhere," said Yaguruma with a mass of cloth in his arms.

The two started carrying in items as they called out "Oof!" and "Hah!" almost to a beat. It was practically a street performance. Once they finished bringing in the items, they organized them on the floor. The two worked in perfect synchronization. Kou felt like they were opening a store right there on the premises.

White Princess and Black Princess were both surprised.

"These are things we might need?"

"I—I have no idea!"

Kou's eyes were wide, too, as he struggled to grasp the situation.

Hikami and Mirei entered the room after Tsubaki and Yaguruma. Mirei closed the door with a soft bump from her bottom.

"Excuse us. We've started festival preparations, so things are going to get busy," she said.

"You guys weren't paying attention yesterday, but we've already decided what we're doing for the festival," said Hikami. "Like Yaguruma said earlier, the whole classroom is in chaos. I hope you don't mind we brought everything here. And we need to talk about our positions—"

"Before that, Hikami…," said Kou.

"Huh?"

"Don't you want to ask about Black Princess?" Kou was nervous. He had absolutely believed they would ask him about his relationship with her. He couldn't believe they would move right to talking about festival preparations like this.

Hikami and Mirei exchanged glances at Kou's question.

As they did, Tsubaki was tossing boxes around, and Yaguruma was neatly stacking cloths.

A little troubled, Hikami and Mirei finally responded.

"Before we ask about your relationship… There's the reason everyone in Pandemonium made it back from the Gloaming alive. You haven't even told us how you did it," said Hikami.

"Urgh," groaned Kou.

"You're surrounded in mysteries. I can't get all hung up on just one of them… Besides…," said Mirei as she moved her eyes toward Black Princess.

She sat, her legs tucked under her, in blank amazement at the action building in the room. Tsubaki cried "Hiyah!" and hurled out the contents of a new box. The items struck Yaguruma directly in the face, half burying him. Black Princess's arms waved about as if she wanted to help him.

Mirei quietly watched and said, "Millennium Black Princess... I mean, Black Princess doesn't seem dangerous anymore. And both White Princess and you swore on your lives, and you're both our good friends. That's enough for us."

"The last time we ran into her, we were enemies. I do want to hear how you came to be on good terms with the queen of the kihei. I bet it's a long story... But you don't have to tell it until you're ready," said Hikami.

"Mirei, Hikami..." Kou held a hand over his heart as they spoke. He squeezed his hand into a fist as his chest filled with warmth.

He appreciated their words.

It was just too complicated to explain the relationship between himself and Millennium Black Princess. The same went for the reason they had survived the Gloaming.

Any explanation of either would have to touch on a number of points he just didn't want to talk about.

Like the fact that, strictly speaking, he wasn't human anymore.

But they said that if he didn't want to talk about it, that was fine.

He was glad for their faith in him. He bowed his head low.

"Thanks, you two... And um, were you the ones doing surveillance last night?"

"No, it was someone else," said Mirei.

"Really? I thought it would have been you two again."

"It was Sasanoe and Shirai."

"Huh?"

Kou couldn't help making a silly sound.

He hadn't thought Sasanoe would be on surveillance. But that could actually have been a stroke of luck, because it meant he had heard Kou and the Princesses' conversation. He would have heard Black Princess crying and saying she wanted to make it up to Pandemonium. That should be enough to show Sasanoe that Black Princess was no longer their enemy.

Kou nodded. Mirei puffed out her chest and said, "More importantly, let's hurry up and decide. We lie in the dark...but we are also students. It might be a lot of trouble, but let's have as much fun as we can!"

"Fun? With what?" asked Kou, his head cocked.

In front of Kou, Tsubaki flung a white cloth over Yaguruma's head, hiding him. He raised his arms and struck a pose like a ghost. White Princess smiled brightly. Black Princess looked confused but imitated Yaguruma by bringing her arms up as well.

Mirei crossed her arms and declared, "It's decided, then."

Beside her, Hikami was nodding.

Mirei continued, as if stating one of the laws of nature.

"The roles you will be playing in the haunted house."

The Bride of Demise

3. MEETING THE SECOND TEACHER

Apparently, Pandemonium had a long-standing tradition regarding festivals.

They always contributed a haunted house.

After all, they were class one hundred, the class that didn't officially exist.

Those students with a kihei Bride were kept in Central Headquarters, separate from their peers. Normally, they weren't in the position to be enjoying something like a festival. But it was also Kagura and his predecessors' policy to provide the members of Pandemonium with as close to a normal school life as they could.

And so they would hide their faces, conceal their identity, and join the festival.

More specifically, they would open a haunted house.

Thinking back, Kou did remember hearing something about this festival tradition.

During his time in the Department of Magic Research, he had heard some rumors that went like this: If you wander through the stalls at the festival, you might find, mixed in among the others, a haunted house of mysterious origin, run by a class no one can identify. If you dare venture inside, you'll get the fright of your life.

In other words, they had a terrifying reputation.

The festival's haunted house was considered one of the Academy's seven great mysteries.

I can't believe Pandemonium runs it..., thought Kou as he shook his head.

He never imagined he'd learn the true nature of one of the seven school mysteries now.

At the same time, he turned his thoughts away from the festival.

I shouldn't be thinking about enjoying myself.

He focused on what was in front of him.

A luxurious carpet covered the floor of the dimly lit hallway, and the walls and window frames were decorated with carvings. The building's interior was imposing and old-fashioned. Or so it looked at first. In fact, 3-D images created by cutting-edge magic crystals took the place of interior decoration. All of it was enveloped in a curtain of darkness as translucent as water.

It was already late at night.

Kou had left his room and was wandering the halls of Central Headquarters.

He already knew that the deeper he went into the building, the sparser the decorations would become, gradually exposing the building's functionality. This place wasn't built just to serve guests.

Crouching low as he sprinted, he passed through the part of the building open to the public.

Then he quickened his pace, heading deeper and deeper inside.

* * *

There was a reason Kou was roaming through the halls of Central Headquarters.

He'd explored the place before, during his fifteen thousand repetitions, in search of a way to suppress Millennium Black Princess's rampaging magic. He had even managed to get his hands on many forbidden books.

This time, however, he wandered through the dark in search of something else.

Something he'd been told echoed in his mind:

"It's about what causes the Gloaming... I think there's a possibility a human might be behind it."

Kagura had said those words immediately after they returned from the Gloaming.

He hadn't followed up with a more concrete explanation, and Kou still hadn't discussed any details with him. It almost seemed like he was avoiding the topic.

It was quite possible Kagura himself didn't have much information yet.

If that was the case, acting now would be foolish. But even so...

No student could have the power to bring about the Gloaming, and Central Headquarters is the empire's only stronghold here. If there's any relevant information hiding in the Academy, it has to be inside, thought Kou as he carried out his endless exploration, night after night.

He wasn't going to let the Gloaming happen again.

He would stop at nothing to prevent it.

The inside of Central Headquarters was far larger than it appeared from the outside. The space had been warped using incredible magic. There were probably some rooms that couldn't even be reached through conventional means.

Currently, Kou was mostly revisiting the places he had already been during these fifteen thousand repetitions. Even so, he ran into many barriers to his progress. All of this was possible only because of his special abilities.

...Beyond this point are a lot of rooms used by Central Headquarters' employees. If I want to get through without being caught, I just need to wait for my chance in fifteen seconds and run for it. That's when everyone will be looking away.

Every time Kou was about to be caught, he just turned back time a little, then searched for a way to overcome the obstacle or an alternative route. That's how he'd managed to acquire the documents of note he'd been after in the past. After he found the information, he would go back in time and sleep.

Now, too, he slipped between the employees like a ghost. He flew down the next hallway like an arrow loosed from a bow. He went to turn a familiar corner.

That's when someone grabbed his arm.

Something cold pressed against his skin.

His throat was slashed from one side to the other.

* * *

"…What would you do if you died instantly like this?" asked a low voice.

After a few seconds, Kou realized he was still alive. His attacker shoved him away.

Kou stared at the person in the dim light. He'd thought his attacker was a man, based on the deep voice, but it was a woman. Her vermillion uniform suited her slim body well. Long copper hair fell down her back. Her eyes were shockingly cold.

She gave the impression of a steel sword, one even more tempered than White Princess.

Then, after a few seconds, Kou reassessed his previous assumption.

This person is a man…probably. No, a woman. Maybe?

He honestly couldn't tell. What's more, he didn't know anything about them, not even their name.

Were they an enemy? Or an ally?

"…Who are you?" asked Kou.

"Considering the situation, that's a pretty stupid question. Zero points. Go home and review your lessons."

Kou furrowed his brow at the odd response. It sounded a bit like something a teacher would say.

Then the person spoke, as if to back up Kou's suspicion.

"My name is Shuu Hibiya. You may find I look like both a man and a woman, but pay that no mind. It's fine that way. Just understand that I am the second teacher of Pandemonium."

"The second?"

Kou frowned. He did remember hearing something from Hikami about two teachers with Princess Series Brides having been sent to defend the imperial capital.

If one of them was here, what did that mean?

"Does that mean you've returned?" asked Kou.

"Yes, finally. Now that the threat of the Gloaming has passed, I was permitted to come see the faces of my darling pupils. I've heard about you, too—that your performance is excellent, but you're not very cute. How unfortunate."

Hibiya, gender unknown, responded without pause.

Kou knitted his brows. Fortunately, they didn't seem to be an enemy. But between Hibiya and Kagura, were all of Pandemonium's teachers this eccentric?

Then Hibiya asked a question that took Kou entirely by surprise.

"You're...repeating time, aren't you?"

"How did you...?" Kou asked stiffly. Aside from White Princess and Black Princess, the only one who knew about his ability was Kagura, and Kou had a hard time believing Kagura would share that with someone else. While he was often thoughtless, he wasn't the kind of person to leak his students' important secrets.

Hibiya shrugged, exasperated. "At least try to lie a little. Your reaction was as good as confirmation."

"You were...bluffing?" asked Kou, his voice tinged with anxiety.

Hibiya shook their head slightly. "Not quite. I guessed based on the absurd report Kagura submitted regarding Pandemonium's safe return from the Gloaming. It attributed the success to Kou Kaguro, White Princess, and the other Phantom Ranks doing their utmost...but surviving that sort of disaster isn't something possible through normal human means. Unless the human in question had experienced that same disaster over and over until they were able to come up with a strategy. Neither Sasanoe, Shirai, nor Yurie have that sort of ability. Which means it must be either White Princess or you."

"That sounds like quite a wild guess."

"I only became certain after meeting you. I could tell from watching you walk down the hall that you have no regard for danger. Yours is the kind of unguarded attitude you could expect from someone who knows they can *do it over* if they nearly die. But..."

Hibiya waved the item they were holding. It was a ruler with rounded corners. They made it disappear as if by sleight of hand, then pulled out a thin-bladed knife, twirling it around.

The blade glinted as Hibiya continued, "So I'll ask again: What would you do if you died instantly?"

Kou swallowed in response. In that case, there would be nothing he could do. Kou Kaguro could travel back in time, but there was one absolute requirement: that he consciously activate his ability.

If he died instantly, he wouldn't have the chance.

He would simply die.

Hibiya let out a heavy sigh. "I knew it. You can't use your ability once you're dead. Which makes it even more dangerous to abuse. You're slowly losing your sense of mortality. And the Central Headquarters isn't as gentle a place as you think it is. There are others besides me who have returned from the imperial capital."

"…Who are they?"

"I imagine you're destined to meet them. But running into them at night in Central Headquarters would put you at a distinct disadvantage. That's why I'm stopping you before that can happen. Your careless actions won't help Pandemonium, and they'll only endanger the Academy. You can't be snooping around Central Headquarters, at least not as you are now."

"But—"

"I hate when students talk back. Inexcusable."

Hibiya twirled the knife again. Their eyes narrowed sharply.

They continued, tone serious.

"Next time, I'll kill you."

Kou bit his lip as he sank into thought.

If he activated his ability now, he could go back and make it so he never encountered Hibiya. But if he did, they would just repeat this conversation the next time he was found.

On top of that, if Hibiya could sense from Kou's attitude that it wasn't their first meeting, that would be the end.

Hibiya would likely kill Kou, without even stopping to have a conversation.

And Kou had understood one thing for certain.

This person is strong… I probably can't take them in a straightforward fight.

And so Kou's investigations were put on hold.

He decided to behave himself until the day of the festival.

The Bride of Demise

4. THE CONFESSION INCIDENT

The days passed by in a flurry.

First, they had to assign positions for the haunted house. Out of all the roles available, Kou chose to play a monster. He'd chosen it because, according to Mirei, it was the easiest.

The heart of Pandemonium's haunted house was the costume team, particularly makeup. Apparently, past classes had even left behind a *Complete Monster Makeup Handbook*. It went into a lot of detail.

"Hee-hee, I can't wait to put my skills to the test. Let me show you what I can do!" cried Mirei before volunteering for the makeup team.

Each person made their decision.

"As you can see, I'm quite good at sewing," said Tsubaki. "Choosing a field you're good at puts you on the road to success."

"...I think the props team has the most need for strong helpers," said Hikami. "But that doesn't mean I can't go around helping the other teams, too."

"Sounds pretty nice, only having to work on the day of the festival... I'll join Kou," said Yaguruma.

And so Tsubaki joined the costume team, Hikami agreed to take care of props, and Yaguruma assumed an acting role.

Sasanoe simply declared them all fools and left the classroom. Things went back to normal after that, and Sasanoe resumed skipping classes. Apparently Shirai, who was helping with props, and Yurie, who was working on costumes, both talked to him frequently, but it seemed like he had no interest in helping prepare for the festival.

"I don't think he likes the idea of a haunted house," mused Tsubaki. "I bet he wanted to open an ice cream stall."

"I doubt that's the case," said Kou, a little frightened by the idea of Sasanoe selling ice cream.

"Hmph" was Tsubaki's only reply. She had already started up her costume work. She sat atop the shoulder of her giant stone golem of a Bride, Doll's Guardian, her needle stitching meticulously. Among all her sewing skills, she was apparently most proficient at making cloth bags that closely resembled the skin of a corpse. Kou would have preferred to never learn about that particular specialty.

"Right," said Kagura. "Um, at this point, the best thing to do is… Ah-ha-ha, I know I say this all the time, but no one's listening to me, are they?!"

Pandemonium didn't generally take their lectures very seriously, but at this moment in particular, everyone was focused on preparing for the festival. Even after Kagura had activated the 3-D projection and started talking, everyone's enthusiasm stayed focused squarely on what they were doing.

It didn't matter if class was in session or not, cloth and thread flashed through the air.

When Shuu Hibiya was giving a lecture, however, everyone listened intently.

Kou finally accepted the truth when he saw them standing at the lectern.

Hibiya really is a teacher…

"I won't go as easy on you as Kagura does. I will mercilessly hound anyone who gets failing marks, even if it's just the academic subjects. If you don't understand something, come and ask me until you do. I will answer all your questions until you've worked it out."

Hibiya's lectures were easy to understand. They spoke harshly but welcomed dedicated students. When some of the students did ask questions, Hibiya provided kind, thorough explanations.

The same went for the practical courses.

Hibiya used their superb physical ability to evade attacks from each Bride and take down the students. The flexibility of their joints was in a class all its own, beyond normal human capability. Each strike from Hibiya was hard and fast, easily overwhelming Kou's fighting experience. On top of that, their feedback on the students' weaknesses was far more generous than Kagura's.

"Those who don't want to die when they're in the thick of it, come get the details from me. I'll happily explain everything."

With the addition of a new teacher, their days were filled with excitement.

Just as Kou was beginning to think things would continue like this until the festival, something happened among his friends.

Someone asked to meet Hikami.

* * *

"What's up?"

"What's happening?"

"...What *is* happening?"

"What's all this about, then?"

"What the heck is going on here?"

"...................................?"

Boing, boing, boing, boing, boing.

Kou, White Princess, Yaguruma, Mirei, Tsubaki, and Black Princess were peering out of the bushes in the courtyard.

On the other end of their collective gaze stood Hikami.

He wasn't in a fight, yet his expression betrayed a nervousness they rarely saw from him.

In front of Hikami stood a girl.

Her hair was done up in double braids, and she had a mature air about her. Kou and the others recognized her.

She was a member of Pandemonium, a Flower Rank.

While Hikami had been helping out the costume team, she'd called him aside. Tsubaki had muttered that she "smelled something brewing!" and their usual group had followed after him.

Hiding beside the others in the bushes, Kou kept glancing toward the sky. Finally, he lowered his voice and whispered, "...Tsubaki, I'm not sure anything's brewing at all here."

"What are you saying? Hikami's so straitlaced, and yet he still agreed to hear this girl out. In a way, this is the biggest incident the Academy has ever seen!"

"You could definitely say that... It's a very interesting situation," said Yaguruma.

"Not you too, Yaguruma... Is it really okay to hide in the bushes and spy on them just because it's interesting?"

"I agree with you, Kou, but I think it would be difficult to leave now without them noticing us," noted Black Princess.

"Ooh, something's happening. We should focus on listening," said White Princess cheerfully.

All of them quickly shut their mouths and made every effort to appear like a perfectly normal piece of shrubbery.

In front of them, the Flower Rank girl was starting to speak. She raised her head, her cheeks flushed crimson. "Um, thank you for everything you did during the Gloaming... If it weren't for you relaying information, we on the medic team wouldn't have been able to do our best."

"Oh, you don't have to thank me for that. We're supposed to help each other out in battle, after all," said Hikami, his one visible eye relaxing into a soft smile.

The girl gazed at him, her face turning an even darker shade of red. She looked away and seemed to fumble for her words.

But her expression showed determination as she continued.

"Hikami, I, um, I really respect you for being so kind and such a good leader. I...really like you. I don't think there's anyone as incredible as you."

"O-oh... Thank you. Not sure I deserve that much praise, though," replied Hikami calmly, though he did look somewhat shaken.

The girl looked away again. She squeezed her hands into fists, then brought them to her chest. Her voice was full of passion, she asked, "Hikami, would you go out with me?"

"Oh no," whispered Kou.

"...That was direct," muttered Yaguruma.

"Oh my," said Mirei.

"Way to go, Hikami," said Tsubaki.

"Kou has me; he would never have an affair!" declared White Princess under her breath.

4. The Confession Incident

"Ooh," said Black Princess, "I don't know what I would do if anyone other than White Princess confessed their love to my Kou…"

While they were working through their confusion in the bushes, the scene in front of them continued to unfold.

It seemed the girl had taken Hikami by surprise. He blinked several times. Then, looking somewhat uncertain, he responded with a question. "You mean…as your boyfriend?"

"What else could she mean, you idiot?!" cried Tsubaki.

"Tsubaki, you're being too loud!" said Kou as he quickly clamped his hands over Tsubaki's mouth.

"Yes…as my boyfriend," said the girl with a nod.

Hikami shook his head, looking embarrassed. "I'm sorry. I can't accept, if that's what you want. I really appreciate it, but a Groom should put his Bride first. Having any other partner would—"

"It's because of Mirei, isn't it?"

"………………………………………………………………What?" Hikami and Mirei said in perfect unison.

Kou and the others turned toward Mirei with considerable apprehension. It appeared that her name coming up in such a situation had struck her like a magic thunderbolt.

Hikami quickly replied to the girl, "No…Mirei has nothing to do with it. Why would you mention her at a time like this?"

"Well, you and Mirei are so close."

"Yeah, but that doesn't mean we have that kind of relationship."

"Then would you be perfectly fine with her dating someone else?"

"Uh……well……"

A mysterious silence descended. Kou and the others held their breath. After a few seconds, Hikami gazed at the sky. A bird flew by high above.

Even he looked bewildered as he said, "I……don't think I would."

"What? He wouldn't?" whispered Mirei in surprise. "Why…?"

Kou and the others exchanged looks. Tsubaki, White Princess, and Black Princess all sported grave expressions. Kou and Yaguruma, in particular, shared a look. They leaned toward each other and started whispering among themselves.

"I heard that Hikami and Mirei weren't dating, but…what if Hikami subconsciously felt… I mean, just maybe, what if?"

"Hmm…just maybe, maybe he does…"

"Hold on, you two, what are you talking about?" asked Mirei, gripping each of their shoulders. They squirmed under the exquisite pain of her fingers digging into their skin.

White Princess raised her hand. Her voice quiet, she cheerfully asked Mirei, "So then, would you be okay with Hikami dating someone else, Mirei?"

"Uh…well… I…wouldn't really, no."

"So just maybe!" said Yaguruma.

"So what?!" cried Mirei, looking as angry as a cat bristling its fur.

To shut them up, she bound not White Princess, but Yaguruma in chains. Something about Yaguruma's face made it look like he was enjoying it. Realizing the situation was getting out of hand in more than one way, Kou rushed to stop them.

And so while they were chattering in the bushes, the girl's confession ended on an ambiguous note.

Kou and the others returned to work, somehow managing to keep Hikami from seeing them.

Despite such an unusual encounter, their days continued as normal.

It was a time of peace they couldn't have imagined during the Gloaming.

And then, finally, the day of the festival arrived.

The Bride of Demise

5. THE FESTIVAL BEGINS

The brick pavement of the square was set in an intricate pattern, and now the glitter of magic overlaid it with a new one. The Music Corps, formed of volunteers, stepped on rainbow rings without one thread out of place.

Magic was used to its fullest for the parade. Flower petals and spirits danced gracefully through the air in time with the music.

Many students were in the area, cheering.

At this point, Kou was very familiar with the Music Corps parade. Their performance would open the festivities.

Kou narrowed his eyes. The parade was brimming with energy. But behind the parade…in the distance, he could see the high-grade magic wall, just as he had once before. Its complex structure looked like it had been made from a fusion of beasts of all types and sizes, and it really did look foul. He was struck again by the fact that this was an enclosed space—and that they were always in danger. But even so, he could feel his excitement about the festival winning out over those other emotions.

He nodded slightly, thinking. *Usually the Gloaming kills 90 percent of Combat students, 60 percent of the entire student population, and all of Pandemonium… And yet…*

He'd managed to reverse fate itself.

Large crowds were passing by him now. Everyone was chatting, laughing, and having fun.

All of those most important to Kou were alive.

As he gazed at the festive sight, he thought deeply about how happy he was.

And most important of all, he had his two Brides beside him.

"This is amazing, Kou," said White Princess. "Festivals are wonderful. This is the first time I've seen the Academy this full of life."

"I can't believe I'm able to stand among such beauty," Black Princess whispered with slight hesitation. "And with Kou, even… It's like a far-off dream. I hope I never wake up, not ever…"

"It's okay, Black Princess! It's not a dream!" replied White Princess cheerfully.

They both were wearing masks: White Princess a rabbit mask, and Black Princess a cat mask.

There was a tradition among the regular students of wearing masks during festivals, copying the style of festivals in the imperial capital. Everyone watching the parade was wearing a mask of their choosing. It was like they were all inhuman creatures. Thanks to this, Kou and the other Pandemonium students were able to walk around without suspicion, despite not belonging to any known department or class.

White Princess was wearing her usual outfit, but she was able appear as just another guest from the imperial capital.

"Are you three having fun?"

"Oh, Mirei," Kou said, raising his head. He was wearing a mask resembling a wolf's head. He turned around to see Mirei standing behind him wearing a fox mask.

Behind her was Hikami with Tsubaki on his shoulders. They wore a goat and bird mask, respectively. Tsubaki's arms were filled with masses of sculpted candy art, ice cream, grilled chicken skewers, and even a glass flute. She must have worked fast; the festival had only just started.

Kou was a little taken aback, but that didn't stop him from greeting them warmly. "You all look like you're enjoying the festival, Tsubaki in particular."

"Of course. Those who enjoy themselves are the real winners of this kind of event," replied Tsubaki.

"And I have absolutely no idea why you're making me carry you on my shoulders," said Hikami. "I feel like a dad, or an older brother, or a grandad, or even a mom."

"I'm not sure how I should feel about you suddenly embracing mother-hood," responded Mirei.

"Ha-ha-ha! So I'm Pandemonium's strong, kind mother?" said Hikami.

"No one said that. And would you want them to?" asked Mirei, engaging in their usual banter.

As they chatted, Kou looked around. He realized one member of their usual group wasn't present. He cocked his head. "Mirei, I don't see Yaguruma."

"Yeah, he's the monster in the haunted house right now. Don't forget what time you're scheduled to take over, Kou. It might slip your mind while you're enjoying the festival."

"I'll be careful."

Kou nodded at Mirei's warning. Each of the actors had a set time they were responsible for in the haunted house. He had to make sure he didn't arrive late for his group's meetup.

Apparently, Mirei had just been over there to check on everyone. According to her, Pandemonium's contribution to the festival was a huge success.

"The whole point of a haunted house is to scare people, after all. I heard plenty of screams coming from the house…"

While the six were talking, the applause around them suddenly grew louder.

Kou looked back to see the Music Corps taking a bow. The last of the spirits made a rainbow in the sky and scattered sparkling petals, their shining gold and silver hues transforming into bubbles in midair before exploding. The spray of light resembled stars as it flew above the audience's heads.

Black Princess applauded, engrossed in the performance. Kou and the others watched her; his eyes filled with joy at the sight.

Mirei clapped her hands together to get everyone's attention. "Our Brides can't appear in front of the regular students, but yours are different. This is a rare opportunity. How about the three of you go on a date?"

"That's a good idea," said Kou. "White Princess, Black Princess, is there anywhere you want to go?"

The two of them turned to each other.

There was a huge variety of stalls and events put together by each class for the festival. There were shops, plays, indoor exhibitions, street performances, singing, and phantom beast shows, just to name a few. The two Princesses probably weren't sure what to choose. Suspecting as much, Kou waited for them to answer.

The two of them blinked. They appeared to be having a silent conversation.

They giggled and nodded to each other, then White Princess said, "I knew it; you are me. It seems we have the same thing in mind."

"Yes, you are definitely me. I don't think there's the slightest difference," replied Black Princess.

Kou tilted his head in confusion. They both turned toward him.

With beautiful smiles, they said:

"We'll go anywhere..."

"...so long as we're with you."

Kou was a little surprised but quickly nodded.

He squeezed his Brides' hands in his, and the three rushed over to the festival.

* * *

Pandemonium had been well compensated after they'd dealt with the Gloaming.

The first thing Kou spent his money on were some adorable frozen treats.

The dessert in question used syrup synthesized from spirits to dye it into the various colors of the changing sky. Lined up at the front of the shop were examples colored with the navy of early dawn, the blue of noontime, the crimson of sunset, and the black of night. All of them were semitransparent and incredibly beautiful.

Without thinking, Kou picked up two of different types. For White Princess, he bought one the color of noon and decorated with cloud-shaped sugar candies. He gave Black Princess one the color of night, decorated with star-shaped sugar art. Each treat matched the eyes of the recipient.

Though they looked different, each tasted the same. Even so, the two Princesses shared with each other.

"The noon one tastes refreshing, while the night one has a deep, rich flavor," said White Princess.

"Perhaps our tongues are being tricked by the different appearances. How strange... Hee-hee, and how interesting," replied Black Princess.

The two smiled in agreement. Then they offered their spoons to Kou for him to have some as well.

The two Princesses took turns feeding Kou a spoonful at a time. He crunched the cold ice. They were right; he got the feeling the noon one had the flavor of a blue sky, while the night one had the flavor of a sky filled with stars.

"Hmm, I do think they taste different," he said. "...How mysterious."

"Right?"

"Indeed."

The three walked on as they ate spoonfuls of the dreamlike dessert.

Eventually, they came across a group of phantom beasts.

It seemed those in the Academy who owned a phantom beast had brought them all together.

The rare creatures were held in a pen.

White Princess ran over and cried, "Aw, look, Kou! They're so cute!"

"Hmm... I've seen them in the ruins, but this is my first time seeing ones kept by humans," said Black Princess.

With the parade and performance over, they were holding a petting zoo, under the supervision of the students running the stall. It made Kou somewhat uneasy, however.

Phantom beasts had good intuition. They might realize that the Princesses were kihei.

But his fears turned out to be unfounded.

"Oh, good girl. She's so well-behaved," said White Princess as she gently petted a gryphon. The eagle-headed creature snuggled sweetly up to her.

Beside her was Black Princess, timidly holding a young fenrir. It seemed like one of the students in charge had held it out to her, and she had just sort of accepted it.

Her legs trembled as she cried, "A-are you sure? It might break in my arms! I'm too scared; I can't look! I can feel its warmth, but what if that's blood?! Kou, is it okay?"

"It's okay, Black Princess. Relax."

"Miss, you're so good at holding him! Take this, too, if you like," said another student as she cheerfully handed Kou a pamphlet. It contained facts on the phantom beasts. This was another part of the festival that really made it feel like a school event.

Kou bowed and accepted the pamphlet.

As he did, he realized something.

The girl handing him the pamphlet was one of his upperclassmen from when he was in Research—and someone who'd helped him out quite a lot.

She had been so kind to him. He remembered her passionately teaching Asagiri all about phantom beasts. Both of them were wearing masks right now, however, and it seemed she hadn't realized who he was.

Kou lowered his head.

"White Princess, Black Princess...let's go."

He took his Brides and left the petting zoo behind.

* * *

Kou and his Brides came to a stop again somewhere along the path. He could hear lively music coming from nearby.

He looked in the direction of the sound and saw spirits in an area marked off by a line, tossing flowers around. It seemed to be an impromptu dance floor. Joyous laughter rang out from here and there.

A lot of the students had taken off their masks, perhaps because they were moving around so much. Drinks were also being sold inside.

Black Princess reacted when she saw the people smiling, drinking, and dancing. Her shoulders trembled like she was itching to join in. White Princess paused in thought for a moment but quickly took Black Princess's hand. She removed both their masks and rushed off.

"Kou, this is a rare opportunity! Let's dance, too!" she said.

"O-oh... You've gotten more assertive since Black Princess arrived," he replied, nodding in approval like a dad or older brother. He temporarily removed his mask as well.

As he did so, the Princesses reached the dance floor. White Princess danced smoothly in time with the music.

"Like this, Black Princess," she said.

"L-like this?"

White Princess took Black Princess's hand and spun her around.

There was no way White Princess could know the correct steps for this particular dance, but when Kou glanced at the others around her, he saw she was perfectly in sync. Black Princess, on the other hand, was lost. She moved her feet desperately, trying to match the steps. It did look like she was slowly catching on.

Once Black Princess had settled into the dance, White Princess ran back over to Kou and curtsied gracefully to him.

"You're next, Kou. May I have this dance?" she asked.

"Yes, White Princess, I would love to dance with you."

She took his hand, and a smile bloomed on her face. They spun two, then three times.

Kou put a hand on her waist. She bent backward in a smooth arc. She took his arms and did an excellent spin before striking a perfect pose. Someone whistled.

Seeming satisfied, White Princess nodded before she ran back over to Black Princess.

"Okay, Black Princess! Go ahead!" she said.

"Uh…? Oh."

White Princess pushed on Black Princess's back, moving her toward Kou.

Black Princess was surprised but took Kou's hand. Her face was bright red as she whispered, "U-uh, Kou… I'm not very good at dancing, but if you'd like to…"

"Of course, Black Princess, I'd love to dance with you."

She spun around, still uncertain. Her black hair sparkled as it formed an arc in the air.

Next, White Princess took Black Princess's hand again. The two twirled around several times, enjoying themselves.

They danced for a while longer, trading off leading or following.

As Kou began to tire out, he went to buy drinks. He brought back three glasses of rose-colored carbonated water. They clinked their glasses together and took a long swig. Both the Princesses started coughing, unused to the carbonation.

Kou smiled as he watched them.

…Ah, I'm so happy.

His feelings were genuine.

* * *

Next, the trio headed for a street lined with stalls.

The colorful signs were packed so tightly they nearly swallowed up the entire road—a flood of things and noise and color. There were a lot of people. The three tightly linked their hands as they passed through so they wouldn't get separated.

Black Princess suddenly stopped in front of a stall with hundreds of wind chimes hung all over it. Her eyes sparkled as she looked at one with a red fish painted on the side.

Kou saw her expression and gently asked, "Do you want it, Black Princess?"

"Oh, no, Kou… I want to leave it here, swimming with its friends," she said with a smile. Her tone was filled with a quiet kindness.

Kou nodded and stroked her head. She pulled her shoulders up in enjoyment.

"Aw, it's not fair if you only stroke Black Princess's head," declared White Princess. "Me too, please."

"Of course, White Princess, It's my pleasure."

Kou stroked White Princess's head as well. She nodded in satisfaction and then stroked Black Princess's head in turn.

The three of them blushed and laughed.

But just then, they heard an angry shout.

"Come on, that can't be right!"

Kou turned around, searching for the source of the voice, his eyes darting back and forth. It seemed like it was coming from in front of a stall with a shooting game. The customer and stall operator were having an argument. It wasn't the sort of disturbance that suited a festival.

Kou furrowed his brow and strained his ears.

It seemed like the problem was that the prizes acting as targets weren't falling.

"Something's fishy. I shot it three times, but it didn't fall!" said the customer, a girl wearing a bird mask.

"I don't know; maybe you just have bad luck," replied the stall operator with a laugh, a boy with a monkey mask.

The furrow in Kou's brow deepened. A lot of money would be changing hands during the festival. Surely some students had planned scam stalls to take advantage of the situation, though it seemed tactless to do so at a festival commemorating their survival of the Gloaming.

"...I can't leave this be," whispered Kou as he started to make his way over.

Just then, a black shadow appeared in front of the stall. With a clatter, the newcomer tossed the operator in the monkey mask some coins.

"Oh, a customer?" he asked. "This much money will buy you...ten shots."

There was a quick rat-a-tat-tat as the gun fired, and *every single one* of the prizes fell.

The shots had been fired rapidly and with precision. The prizes struck took the remaining ones with them. It was like a typhoon had hit the stall.

"...Uh, what the...?"

The boy working the stall was struck dumb. As he stood in a daze, the student in black bent down to pick up the stuffed animal that had been at the center of the argument. He handed it to the girl in the bird mask.

"...Here," he said.

"Ah, s-seriously? ...Thank you," she said.

"Don't thank me. Scams like this just piss me off," muttered the boy in black from behind his crow mask.

The boy in the monkey mask was about to argue back, but the student in black glared at him, and he fell silent. Without another word, the student in black turned to walk away, his coat swirling.

Kou couldn't help crying out. "Sasanoe!"

"Hmm, Kou? What?" asked Sasanoe, but Kou didn't actually have anything to say to him.

At a loss for words, Kou glanced to Sasanoe's side. There he found Crimson Princess, just as he'd expected.

She was one of the Princess Series and Sasanoe's beautiful Bride.

She looked to be in a good mood. Kou could see a spark of joy in her normally expressionless eyes. Her arms were filled with various festival goodies—a sunset-colored dessert, water balloons, stuffed animals, and exquisitely crafted candies. Sasanoe had probably bought all of them for her.

It was a little surprising to see the two most powerful members of Pandemonium enjoying the festival so heartily.

"A-are you having fun?" asked Kou.

"Not really," said Sasanoe.

"Even now?"

"Crimson Princess is the one enjoying herself. Though, festivals aren't bad, I suppose. They boost morale for the next fight," Sasanoe said flatly.

Kou found himself agreeing. There was value in celebrating their survival of the Gloaming. He understood that value better than anyone after his fifteen thousand trips through hell.

The two Phantom Rank Grooms nodded in firm agreement.

Then, suddenly, a familiar voice pierced through the hustle and bustle of the crowd.

"Ah, there you are!" shouted Kagura. "Sasanoe! You're the only one without a role! Go be a monster! Also, come to class sometimes!"

"Kagura… That fool…," said Sasanoe, before dashing off with Crimson Princess. They disappeared into the crowd, and Kagura chased after them, his coat flapping in the wind. It didn't look like he had any intention of giving up.

"Come oooon! Fine, be like that… But I'm not letting you get away!"

"Give it your best shot."

At first glance, this might look like a game, but they were the most powerful student and teacher in the Academy, and this game of tag was no joke.

The two disappeared with incredible speed.

Kou watched them go. "I'm scheduled to play the monster, too…," he said. "So let's see as much as we can before then. It occurred to me when I saw Crimson Princess…but is there anything the two of you want? Just tell me, if so."

"Well, Kou!" said White Princess. "If it's all right, I want one of those glass flutes that Tsubaki had!"

"I was…um…interested in those candies," Black Princess joined in. "They were so delicate…and beautiful. I can't stop thinking about them."

"Okay, then let's look for the stalls selling them."

Kou agreed to his Brides' wishes with a smile.

The three enjoyed the festival, right up until the very last moment.

* * *

Eventually, it was time for Kou to take over playing the haunted house monster.

Meanwhile, the Princesses would be responsible for drawing in customers. White Princess held aloft a sign featuring a surprisingly cute-looking illustration. Black Princess, on the other hand, had lowered her face.

"Okay, Kou! We'll work hard!" said White Princess.

"I'm not sure this is a suitable job for me...," said Black Princess. "Won't I just scare them off?"

"It's okay, Black Princess," White Princess assured her. "You are me, and I am you. There's nothing to worry about."

Then the two joined hands and ran off.

Kou waved after them until they disappeared into the distance.

Just then, something dawned on him. Even with the masks on, it was easy to tell those two were beautiful. Wasn't there something tragic about them enchanting students and drawing them into a haunted house?

But well... That's part of the fun of the festival.

He nodded to himself and turned his thoughts toward his current role.

Circling around the haunted house to the back door, he headed to the meeting spot. There he found Yaguruma waiting to switch out with him, standing in a daze. He looked completely worn-out. There was an almost picturesque quality to the melancholy coloring of his androgynous features. That said, something seemed off about him.

Tilting his head to the side, Kou asked, "Hey, Yaguruma. Looks like you worked pretty hard out there."

"Ah...Kou...?"

Yaguruma looked up. Kou took the costume from him. It was a cloth sack Tsubaki had put her every effort into making look like the rotting face of a corpse.

Then, once Yaguruma had passed the torch on to Kou, he said, "Listen, the important thing is to take on the monster's feelings... Feel the monster's hatred of humans, its desire to bring calamity to the world... If you do that, you'll naturally draw out humanity's screams."

"Wait a second, Yaguruma, aren't you getting a little too into this?" asked Kou, flustered. Yaguruma was clearly not in a good state. A creepy chuckle escaped his delicate, beautiful face.

Then he gave Kou a thumbs-up and wobbled off on unsteady feet.

Kou was bewildered. *What was that all about?*

But he did what was expected of him and entered the haunted house's dressing room.

* * *

It was there that he finally understood Yaguruma's transformation.

It was the direct result of the makeup team's fiery enthusiasm.

"I don't have enough pigment for the ulcers on the hands!"

"You're being too hesitant with your shadows! With work like this, we can't expect the customers to shudder and scream with fright!"

"Everyone knows those who underestimate the haunted house will be the first to die!"

"Okay, listen. You are now a monster. You have become a monster. Your ultimate purpose is to scare. You exist only to strike fear in the hearts of humans. Don't forget."

That last part was a warning from Mirei.

And Kou's brainwashing didn't stop there.

You are a monster. You have become a monster.

No, wait—you have always been a monster.

You were a monster from the moment you were born.

Once the brainwashing had fully taken hold, Kou was released into the haunted house.

Pandemonium had constructed a small shed for their performance. It looked poor and run-down on the outside, but the inside utilized as much magic technology as possible. The dimly lit space mixed with 3-D projections was perfect for heightening the visitors' fear.

Customers would rush, frightened and out of breath, into the deepest reaches of the structure, where Kou would appear and charge after them.

If he used his full power, he could easily outpace the movements and speed of an average human.

In other words, he looked positively monstrous.

Most of their visitors screamed in genuine terror and tripped over themselves running out.

Thus, Kou was able to throw dozens of people into the depths of despair—proof that his mind and body had completely morphed into those of a monster. But what else could you expect? Kou had been a monster from the moment he was born.

As he fell deeper into the role, he began to lose his sense of humanity entirely.

But just then, his movements came to a stop.

"Oooh, it's scary... I'm so scared. I can't take this anymore. Why'd I even come in here? I can't believe I got separated from everyone... Where'd they all go?"

Someone was crying. But the real problem was their voice.

Kou recognized it.

Disbelief kept him frozen to the spot.

He hesitated to leap out in front of her. He didn't think she would recognize him dressed as a monster, but he didn't want to scare her.

Uncertain what to do, he took a step back.

As he did, his foot knocked against a fake tree that was part of the set.

There was a clatter.

"Wh-what was that? Is someone there? Rei?" said the girl, calling the name of one of her friends. She stepped closer, completely unguarded. She didn't seem to suspect there might be a monster waiting ahead of her. She was always so trusting.

Kou panicked, but there was nowhere nearby to hide.

The girl stepped right up to him. She'd removed her mask, perhaps because she had been crying. She blinked. Her large chestnut-colored eyes complemented her short brown hair.

It was Asagiri Yuuki, his former classmate from the Department of Magic Research.

Finding a monster before her, she was just about to scream. But Kou spoke up without thinking. "D-don't be scared; it's okay."

"Huh...? That voice..."

Her response surprised Kou. He hadn't thought she would be able to tell who he was just from his voice. But she instantly leaned forward.

Her eyes shone brightly.

Without a shred of hesitation, she reached out her hand and grabbed the sack covering Kou's face.

Then she smoothly yanked the head from the rotting corpse before her, exposing the face within.

Not knowing what else to do, he called her name.

"Asa...giri..."

"I knew it was you, Kou!" cried Asagiri, stretching out her arms.

Then she caught him in a very vigorous hug.

He fell backward, taking the fake tree with him and causing a horrible racket.

Even then, Asagiri didn't let go. Her voice grew louder, and she started sobbing.

"Kou! It's really you... You're alive!"

Large tears streamed down her face as she kept squeezing the monstrous "corpse" in her arms.

The Bride of Demise

6. A LONG-AWAITED REUNION

Kou's thoughts turned back to the day of the entrance ceremony.

Many of the new students were trembling with nervousness or even crying. Lined neatly in their rows, they were engulfed in despair and confusion.

Kou was the only one who wasn't bothered.

After the strict and austere ceremony, he made his way to the buildings that housed their classes.

That's when someone suddenly called out to him.

"You're not afraid, are you? I'm jealous."

Kou turned back. There was a petite girl standing right beside him.

He looked into her eyes and saw she was frightened. And that's why he answered her.

"No, I'm not afraid. I don't mind joining you, if it'll make you feel better."

He held out his hand to her. She blinked as she took it and said, *"You're sweet."*

"I just thought it'd be nice if I could help a bit. I don't think that counts as being sweet," replied Kou, and the girl smiled. Then she told him her name.

"I'm Asagiri. Asagiri Yuuki."

The two of them had been friends ever since.

She was a kind girl. When they went on dangerous research missions, she always prayed for his safety, in addition to her own. She had the modest dream of owning a phantom beast one day. Back then, he had been

labeled a white mask due to his emotionless demeanor, but she paid that
no mind and stuck with him anyway.

And then came that fateful day when they were investigating the outside.
The day when Kou and Asagiri were *separated by death*.

"Scatter!"
Once he had made up his mind to act as bait for the Special Type kihei,
he had shouted the command.
Like tiny spiders running out from their mother, the crowd of students
dashed away. Only Asagiri had tried to run toward him, but Isumi had
dragged her away.
Once they were a safe distance away, in a voice so quiet the two of them
couldn't hear, Kou murmured, "Take care."
He gave a small quick wave.
The sight of the flower petals at the ceremony and Asagiri's smile crossed
his mind briefly.

That had been the end.
That was when Kou's and Asagiri's fates split forever.
They would never meet again.
Kou had accepted that.

* * *

"Kou, Kou… Ooooh, Kou… I'm so glad…"
But now, Kou was wrapped in Asagiri's arms, with no end in sight.
She still hadn't let go, apparently concerned he might disappear again.
Obviously, they couldn't have their long-awaited reunion unfold in the
depths of a haunted house.
Kou explained the situation to Mirei and the others, and they let him
take a break from his role as the monster.
Somehow, they'd gotten Sasanoe to take his place.
They'd even managed to brainwash him, too.

And so the most powerful monster in the whole haunted house burst
onto the scene.

*   *   *

For Kou, however, a bizarre situation was unfolding.

"...Kou, my dear, who is this girl clinging so close to you?"

"Yes...Kou. Who is this girl clinging to you? She is neither White Princess nor me."

The two Princesses interrogated him, looking unhappy.

They'd been in the middle of drawing in customers to the haunted house, but now they stood stock-still, arms crossed over their chests.

Asagiri's eyes also grew round at the sight of the other two girls. Still hugging Kou's shoulders, she asked, "K-Kou, um, who are they? And more importantly, how are you alive? The upperclassmen said you died. In the ruins. They said we couldn't even recover your body. They told me to give up. But you're alive! I never stopped believing... But why haven't you come to see me? What are you doing now? And why were you in that haunted house? Kou, what's going on?"

"A-Asagiri...," stammered Kou. "I know it's all really confusing, but please calm down."

Asagiri nodded her understanding but stubbornly refused to move away from him. She clung to him tightly, like a child.

White Princess frowned. Trying to be patient, she said, "She seems like a school friend of Kou's. I don't want to be annoying. Friendships among students are important, too. I'm just not sure what to say about something like this, as your Bride..."

"B-bride? Kou, did you get married?" asked Asagiri.

"I-it's hard to explain... Asagiri, let's go somewhere else."

Kou had determined they wouldn't be able to settle things like this.

He excused himself from the Princesses and headed away with Asagiri. The festival hubbub continued.

They slipped through the crowds, looking for someplace quiet.

* * *

Eventually, Kou and Asagiri came out behind the Academy.

They were surrounded by gentle rolling hills covered in thousands of graves.

Each was a testament to someone's death, standing under a clear blue sky. This place was a communal cemetery to remember those who died in the Gloaming.

You might say this was the place farthest removed from the festival.

Kou bowed to a nearby grave, then turned back to face Asagiri before beginning his explanation.

"Asagiri, the truth is: I didn't die back then."

He told his story, leaving out a few details.

He explained how he had been saved by White Princess in the ruins, that they were lucky to make it back to the Academy, that his safe return had resulted in him being transferred, and that he was now living in a different dorm.

He kept the existence of Pandemonium and the Brides a secret. The majority of students in the Academy had lost their families to kihei. They couldn't allow information about Pandemonium to be leaked to the general population.

Asagiri didn't seem satisfied with the explanation but did accept most of it.

Hesitantly, she asked, "So you won't be coming back to Research?"

"No, I can't... Sorry, Asagiri."

"What department are you in now? Can I come visit?"

"They don't openly recruit students. They only bring in people who managed to survive an encounter with a kihei in the depths of the ruins... Would you believe me if I said it's partly to help us recover emotionally? I'm fine now, but a lot of my classmates are pretty fragile. We can't allow visitors from other departments... I'm really sorry."

He was piling lies on top of lies.

Asagiri hung her head and bit her lip. She was clearly suspicious, but she ultimately seemed to accept his story as truth. It was proof of how rare it was for someone to return alive from the depths of the ruins.

Eventually, she stopped asking questions.

With tears in her eyes, she whispered, "I...I always regretted it. I regretted not being able to go to you when you told me to run away."

"You don't need to feel that way. I made my own decision... There's nothing for you to regret."

"That's not true. I'm a coward. Why couldn't I stop Isumi from holding me back? I've been thinking about it ever since... This whole time..."

A tear ran down her cheek. She quietly sobbed. A long silence followed; eventually, she covered her face and took a few deep breaths.

After a while, she managed to say, "Thank you for being alive; thank you so much."

"Asagiri…"

Kou struggled with conflicting emotions. During his fifteen thousand repetitions, he'd cut out his time with Asagiri, thinking it was of no use to him. He'd omitted her, ignored her, denied her.

Now he felt with every fiber of his being how cruel he'd been.

Asagiri was always so kind.

Once, she'd been like a symbolic representation of peace to him.

After he'd joined Pandemonium, he'd become something entirely different from her. But he was still happy to see her again. She really was a dear friend.

He was fully convinced that he should not have cut her out of his life.

Asagiri wiped her tears away and, for some reason, corrected her posture before asking her next question. "So who were those, um, Brides from before?"

"Uh, about that…" Kou thought quickly. Several excuses came to mind, but he couldn't bring himself to say any of them out loud. Eventually, he shook his head. "No, I can't! I don't want to lie about them."

Asagiri stood in front of him, waiting for his answer. He felt a certain embarrassment telling her this, but he forced those feelings aside and spoke seriously.

"…They are both very precious to me. They're something like my fiancées."

"What?!"

Asagiri was taken aback. Fresh shock filled her eyes. Kou pressed a hand to his forehead, feeling a pinch of regret. Embarrassment began to well up inside him.

He closed his eyes as if trying to endure a headache, but this really wasn't something he could lie about.

White Princess and Black Princess are my precious Brides… To lie about—

That's when it happened.

He felt a burning sensation in his abdomen.

Kou Kaguro opened his violet eyes.

He looked down at his chest.

The hilt of a knife protruded from his uniform. Blood dripped slowly from the end.

With each beat of his heart, the hilt twitched up and down. The blood running along its length looked terribly vivid. The long blade was embedded completely in his chest.

Intense pain struck him, and he knew.

He'd been stabbed.

He slowly looked up and asked the person in front of him:

"...Why?"

There was no response. Asagiri just smiled vaguely back at him.

He had never imagined she might kill him. He thought they'd had a good relationship. But at the same time, he thought:

It makes sense she would kill me.

During his fifteen thousand repetitions, Asagiri was the one he had treated most cruelly. But there was no way she could know that. He had no idea what had motivated this act of violence.

But he didn't have time to think about that.

She grabbed the hilt of the knife, twisted it, then pulled the blade from his chest.

It gouged a hole in his guts. Blood spilled to the ground.

His vision wavered from the shock.

The scenery of the Academy around him shook and swam.

His body leaned forward, and he collapsed.

The very last image to surface in his mind was that of two beautiful figures, one white, one black. He recalled the smiles of his Brides and clung to the memory.

He was dying.

In that moment, he concentrated and closed his eyes.

And he traveled back in time, to before he was killed.

The applause around them suddenly grew louder.

Kou looked back to see the Music Corps taking a bow. The last of the spirits made a rainbow in the sky and scattered sparkling petals, their shining gold and silver hues transforming into bubbles in midair before exploding. The spray of light resembled stars as it flew above the audience's heads.

Black Princess applauded, engrossed in the performance. Mirei and the others watched her; their eyes filled with joy at the sight.

He'd returned to the start of the festival.

"…What's wrong, Kou? Your face is all stiff," said White Princess.

"Uh…," he said, rubbing his cheek.

Why had he been stabbed? Why had he almost been killed?

His thoughts raced, but no answer came to him.

Eventually, he responded.

"…It's nothing."

The Bride of Demise

7. IT MAKES SENSE

There were many different kinds of glass flutes.

White Princess chose one in the shape of a small bird. She brought her mouth to its blue tail and blew air through it, producing a clear note. She skillfully played the lullaby that Kou had sung to her before.

Black Princess and Kou closed their eyes in enjoyment as they listened to the pleasant melody.

"What do you think?"

"It was wonderful, White Princess."

"A beautiful sound. I'm amazed you can play it so well."

The two gave her a small round of applause.

She bowed and smiled.

There were also various kinds of crafted sweets.

After a long, difficult deliberation, Black Princess chose an exquisite work of art in the shape of a white snake. She liked how gracefully it seemed to rise into the blue sky. She clutched the candy-filled bag to her chest.

"It's so beautiful...and the color is like White Princess."

"You're right, it's the exact color of her hair."

"What's this about? You're making me blush."

Black Princess said she would keep the candy in their room for a while as a decoration.

White Princess wholeheartedly approved.

*   *   *

The two Princesses held the precious gifts Kou had bought them in their arms. It was as if they were admiring the greatest treasures in the world.

Kou nodded as he watched them, pleased that they were happy.

At the same time, he could feel a pain in his abdomen where he hadn't yet been stabbed.

* * *

Kou didn't particularly change what he did his second time through the festival.

They went where they wanted to go and saw what they wanted to see. Kou let his Brides enjoy themselves to the fullest.

But he was still mulling over what had happened.

I don't understand why Asagiri tried to kill me.

He couldn't fathom her motive. But that didn't change the fact that she had done it.

He had a strong desire to ask her why, but he couldn't just go up and question her. He also didn't want to wait until she was about to kill him, stop her, and then ask. He was afraid to hear her real intentions. If things went badly, something precious to him might be smashed to pieces. The most peaceful solution he could find was to do everything in his power to avoid her.

That should prevent anything from happening, for now.

Kou had come to a conclusion. That was enough for now, and it would prevent the festival from being ruined.

He had made his decision.

I have to make sure I don't run into Asagiri.

"Hurry, Kou," urged White Princess. "You have to play the monster soon. We need to see everything we want to before then."

"Oh, I heard beautiful singing... What if we go that way? I...I like songs, too," said Black Princess.

"Okay, let's do that."

Kou ran through the bustle of the festival with his two Brides at his side.

But its lively sounds seemed somehow distant to him.

* * *

Kou kept thinking.

Why had Asagiri stabbed him?

Why had she tried to kill him?

But no matter how much he thought and thought, no answers came.

Right now, the Princesses were enjoying the singing.

The song was an opera, with layered voices telling a story. Black Princess, in particular, seemed caught up in the unfolding world of the song.

While they listened, Kou kept thinking on his own. But unable to reach a conclusion, he shook his head.

He'd slipped deep into thought when someone said his name.

"Kou."

He felt a sudden tap on his shoulder and turned around to see what it was.

Beside him stood only White Princess. He couldn't see Black Princess anywhere.

Kou cocked his head, wondering if Black Princess had gotten lost. Before he could ask, however, White Princess spoke.

"Black Princess said you seemed worried about something and asked me to talk to you about it since you and I are more familiar with each other."

"Black Princess said that? Where is she?"

"Don't worry. She and I caught Sasanoe and Crimson Princess as they were walking through the street with all the stalls. She's with them, just in case something happens and there's trouble. It would be a lie to say Sasanoe was happy to help…but he agreed because he could tell Black Princess was worried."

"Really? …With Sasanoe…"

Before, Sasanoe had attacked Black Princess in the classroom, but it looked like his animosity toward her had already vanished. Kou was relieved to hear that.

Standing in front of him, White Princess puffed up her chest and said, "Which means, Kou, you can talk to me about anything that's bothering you, okay?"

"White Princess… Thank you. But I don't really understand it myself yet."

He shook his head.

As they talked, the singing changed. The volunteer opera singers stepped off the stage and were replaced with some people carrying instruments. They started to play a slow, beautiful song.

Several boys and girls started to sway as they listened to the music, their bodies pressed against each other.

Though the air was filled with sweet sounds, White Princess frowned gravely.

"You can't even tell me the gist of the problem?" she asked.

"Not yet; I think you'll get angry if I do."

"Kou, you're always like this, even though I'm your wings."

Her blue eyes clouded over. Kou looked away, feeling guilty. But he wanted to avoid White Princess and Asagiri getting into a fight until he understood what was going on. It would be hard to stop that from happening if he told White Princess everything now, when he still didn't have a clue. He had to keep it to himself.

The flow of the music changed again.

A gentle melody drifted to his ears.

"…Kou."

"…Hmm?"

White Princess pulled her mask aside and pressed her lips to his cheek.

There was a softness and a heat, then the sensation faded away.

Kou blinked a few times.

White Princess looked away, her hair swaying. Her cheeks were tinged pink.

She squeezed his hand tight and said, "I love you. I am always with you. Please don't ever forget that."

"…I won't."

Kou moved his hand.

Those white fingers… He could finally reach them after fifteen thousand repetitions.

He squeezed them back.

"I won't forget. Not ever."

The song ended, leaving a heartrending note lingering in the air.

Kou and White Princess walked quietly away.

* * *

After that, they met up with Black Princess to find she was holding some baked treats. Apparently, Sasanoe had bought them for her. Beside her was Crimson Princess, biting into a doll-shaped stuffed pancake with sugar sprinkled on top. Black Princess hesitated at first but nodded in enjoyment once she bit into one.

Sasanoe stood watching them, silently crossing his arms. It really did appear that, since the second exam, he no longer bore her any hostility.

Kou bowed his head to Sasanoe.

"Thank you for looking after Black Princess."

"Don't thank me, fool. It's just a pancake," replied Sasanoe with his usual unimaginative insult.

For a time, they enjoyed the peaceful moment. But eventually, Kagura appeared out of nowhere, dragging Sasanoe into another game of tag.

It seemed no matter how much Sasanoe struggled, he couldn't escape his fate.

Kou also had something he needed to do. His responsibilities hadn't changed since last time.

"Listen, the important thing is—"
"To take on the monster's feelings, right?"

Kou finished Yaguruma's line smoothly and took over the role of monster.

This time, too, he was subjected to the makeup team's brainwashing before being thrown into the labyrinth.

Kou shrugged, resigned to his fate. The only objective for those playing the monster was to scare the living daylights out of the customers. But just as before, focusing on it was quite the mental strain. Kou didn't want to cause trouble for Pandemonium, however, so he put his all into the job.

He kept his cool and fulfilled his responsibility.

The customers ran off in all directions, and he chased them around as necessary.

Finally, the fateful juncture arrived.

"Oooh, it's scary... I'm so scared. I can't take this anymore. Why'd

I even come in here? I can't believe I got separated from everyone...
Where'd they all go?"

...*Asagiri!*

He carefully hid from her, crouching behind a fake tree, being careful not
to make a sound. Instead of jumping out to scare her, he held his breath.

He waited for what seemed like an eternity.

Finally, Asagiri passed him by.

He stepped out from the shadow of the fake tree and watched her go.
He nodded and wiped the sweat from his brow using the cloth mask over
his face.

"Good... I managed to survive for now."

"Hey... That voice..."

Suddenly, someone called out to Kou from behind.

He spun around, and a hand grabbed the cloth mask over his head.

Without a moment's notice, the person pulled off Kou's costume, forcefully revealing his face.

After the sudden act of violence, a boy said, "Huh, it's really you, isn't
it, Kou?"

"...Isumi?" Kou asked, surprised.

Standing in front of him was another classmate from his time in
Research.

It was Isumi Hiiragi, looking at Kou like he'd just seen a ghost.

* * *

Isumi was calmer than Asagiri had been.

He agreed to wait near the exit of the haunted house until Kou was
done with his turn as the monster.

Kou kept working until nearly the end of the festival. He was eventually replaced by Sasanoe, who'd once again been captured. Kou then
explained what was going on to the Princesses and headed outside.

"Sorry for the wait," said Kou.

"...Mm."

Isumi nodded and immediately started walking. He'd taken off his
mask. Perhaps it had gotten stuffy.

Without the mask in the way, Kou could see the familiar furrow in Isumi's brow. It was noticeably deeper today.

The Music Corps was starting another parade in the square. This time, the magic over the bricks wasn't rainbow, but like sparkling stars. This performance seemed to be marking the end of the festival. The music was gentle and elegant.

Isumi glanced sideways at the performance and said, "The girls really like this kind of thing. You always watched it with Asagiri, didn't you?"

"Yeah... But to be honest, I wasn't all that interested myself."

"Yeah? I figured as much."

They kept walking. Feathers and countless bubbles floated through the sky.

It was like a beautiful dreamscape.

Students gathered around, drawn by the sight.

Isumi walked away, trying to escape the growing crowd. He slipped between the permanent café and weapon shop, heading farther back. The cheers grew quieter in the distance as they continued.

Eventually, Isumi leaned back against a dingy wall.

In a gruff tone, he said, "All right. Why the hell are you alive, white mask?"

"About that..."

Feeling a little nostalgic at the old insult, Kou began his story. He told Isumi the same thing he had told Asagiri. Once Kou finished speaking, Isumi gave an exaggerated grimace.

Isumi seemed entirely unconvinced. "I don't believe it... Who would buy a story like that?"

"...Asagiri, maybe?"

"Yeah, she would. She's too trusting."

A few moments of silence passed. Isumi seemed uncertain what to do.

Kou noticed but didn't press him. He simply waited for his response.

After a while, Isumi scratched his head roughly and said, "...If that's your story, then it's obvious you've got your reasons, whatever they are."

"I appreciate it."

"...Sorry."

"Huh? For what?"

The honest question slipped out of Kou's mouth. He couldn't think of anything Isumi should apologize for.

Isumi's expression shifted instantly. He looked upset. The furrow in his brow grew even deeper. His eyes narrowed in anger, and he started yelling so forcefully spittle flew from his mouth.

"Don't pretend you didn't save my life! And after I said all those things about you…!"

"…But that was something I did on my own… And actually, I should be thanking you."

"For what?"

"For getting Asagiri out of there."

Kou gave Isumi a proper bow of his head.

They were talking about when Kou had decided to act as bait for the Special Type kihei. Kou had asked Isumi to make sure Asagiri got out, and despite the suddenness of the request, Isumi had followed through. He had kept his promise.

Kou was honestly grateful, but Isumi clicked his tongue in annoyance.

Completely disgusted, Isumi asked, "Are you really saying that to the guy who ran away knowing you would be killed?"

"Well, but you kept your promise. That's all that matters."

"…Hmm."

Isumi's anger suddenly faded. He shook his head a few times. Then he gritted his teeth and said, "It's good…that you're alive."

"Isumi…"

Kou was a little surprised. Isumi wasn't a bad person, but he still hadn't expected him to be happy that Kou was alive. Isumi seemed embarrassed as he swept his fingers through his black hair. He looked away, making no attempt to hide the gesture.

Kou thanked Isumi again. "Thank you. It makes me happy to hear you're glad."

"I wouldn't say I'm glad."

"And, Isumi… There's something I want to ask you."

He should be able to ask him now.

With that thought in mind, Kou forced the conversation toward a certain topic.

A loud cheer erupted from the square.

It sounded like the parade was reaching its finale. The wind had even carried some feathers in between the buildings.

Gold flitted through Kou's field of vision as he said, "It's about Asagiri. Has there been anything off about her lately?"

"Asagiri? No, not really…"

The sound of applause faded.

The festival was over.

That's when it happened.

He felt a burning sensation in his abdomen.

Kou Kaguro opened his violet eyes.

He looked down at his chest.

The hilt of a knife protruded from his uniform. The long blade was embedded completely in his chest. The hilt was twisted, gouging a hole in his guts.

Intense pain struck him, and he knew.

He'd been stabbed.

He slowly looked up and asked the person in front of him:

"…Why?"

There was no response. Isumi just looked at him, expressionless.

He had never imagined Isumi might kill him. But at the same time, he thought:

It makes sense he would kill me.

During his fifteen thousand repetitions, he had been cruelest regarding his time in Research. But there was no way Isumi and the others could know that. He had no idea what had motivated this act of violence.

Isumi forcefully pulled the blade from Kou's chest.

Hot drops of blood splattered over his feet.

His vision wavered from the loss of blood.

The scenery of the Academy around him shook and swam.

His body leaned forward, and he collapsed.

He was dying.

In that moment, he concentrated and closed his eyes.

And he traveled back in time, to before he was killed.

The applause around them suddenly grew louder.

Kou looked back to see the Music Corps taking a bow. The last of the spirits made a rainbow in the sky and scattered sparkling petals, their shining gold and silver hues transforming into bubbles in midair before exploding. The spray of light resembled stars as it flew above the audience's heads.

Black Princess applauded, engrossed in the performance. Mirei and the others watched her; their eyes filled with joy at the sight.

He'd returned to the start of the festival.

"...What's wrong, Kou? Your face is all stiff," said White Princess.

"Uh...," he said, rubbing his cheek.

Why had he been stabbed? Why had he almost been killed?

His thoughts raced, but no answer came to him.

Eventually, he responded.

"...I need to go further back."

The Bride of Demise

8. MEETING THE PUPPETS

"I commend you for choosing the costume team. Needlework is good practice for your mental focus," said Tsubaki. She was seated in front of Kou, her chest puffed out in pride, the dexterous movements of her hands holding the needle never ceasing.

Kou was sewing together multicolored cloth that Tsubaki had thrown at him. It wasn't going very well, though. He was having a particularly difficult time with the final steps that were meant to really bring out the creepiness.

Tsubaki winked. "The trick is to sew it crudely on purpose."

They were preparing for the festival.

Kou had traveled back to this point in time and chose to be on the costume team.

This was to avoid the one in a million chance of running into either Asagiri or Isumi.

They'd both killed him, for reasons unknown. Both times had been sudden, unexpected acts of violence.

It's just too weird...

Kou had begun to suspect there might be something strange happening in the background. He needed to get confirmation. But first, he wanted to see what would happen if he didn't run into either of them. If he lived, then the source was somewhere within Asagiri and Isumi.

I'll investigate the two of them once I survive the festival.

Kou stifled his unease. He gripped the cloth tight.

Just then, someone lightly smacked Kou on the head.

"Ow!"

"Why are you zoning out over there, Kou? You'll prick your fingers if you don't watch what you're doing," chided Tsubaki from her seat atop Doll's Guardian's knee.

After reprimanding Kou, she picked up the cloth she'd finished and lined it up along with the others on top of her Bride's head. Doll's Guardian seemed pleased with this situation, despite the fact that he could no longer see.

Tsubaki stroked his hard cheek with her small hand and said in a sweet voice, "You can always talk to me, if there's something bothering you."

"...Huh?" asked Kou.

"What's with that response? I'm still the upperclassman here. You should show a little more respect. And you could rely on others more, too. What I'm trying to say is: You're the biggest idiot ever."

Her jade-colored eyes gazed at him calmly.

Her tone was teasing, but she seemed upset, too. "You take on far too much by yourself. You should tell me right away when you're having trouble."

"Tsubaki... I appreciate it, but right now, I can only accept the sentiment."

Kou bowed his head slightly, and Tsubaki snorted in frustration. She stopped pushing the topic, however, instead turning back to focus on her sewing.

He needed more information before he could rely on others. Tsubaki didn't even know he could travel back in time, so he couldn't very well tell her he was going to suddenly be stabbed by someone he knew.

His hands clenched into fists.

It's still too soon. I still—

Tsubaki smacked him on the forehead again, since he had stopped working.

Actually, there were more than just the two of them at work. Cloth and thread danced around them. Even nails and wood flew through the air.

"Aw, come on, guys! Why am I even talking if you never listen?!"

No one listened to Kagura.

Everyone knew.

The festival was close at hand.

* * *

The Music Corps' parade opened the festival.

Kou gazed at the magic wall beyond them.

Its complex structure looked like it had been made from a fusion of beasts of all types and sizes, and it really did look foul. He was struck again by the fact that this was an enclosed space—and that they were always in danger. He could feel a sense of disquiet winning out over his excitement about the festival.

Something's happening… But I don't know what that something is.

As he gazed at the festive sight, he bit down hard on his lip. That's when he heard her.

"Are you three having fun?"

"Oh, Mirei."

He turned around to see Mirei standing behind him wearing a fox mask.

Behind her was Hikami with Tsubaki on his shoulders. Seeing the two, he said the same thing he had the last time.

"You all look like you're enjoying the festival, Tsubaki in particular."

"Of course. Those who enjoy themselves are the real winners of this kind of event," replied Tsubaki.

While the six were talking, the applause around them suddenly grew louder.

Kou looked back to see the Music Corps taking a bow. Black Princess clapped her hands, engrossed in the performance.

Mirei clapped her hands together to get everyone's attention. "Our Brides can't appear in front of the regular students, but yours are different. This is a rare opportunity. How about the three of you go on a date?"

"Actually, I have a different suggestion. How about we look around the festival together as a group?" suggested Tsubaki.

This hadn't happened last time. Kou blinked, thrown off guard by her suggestion.

She bit into one of her chicken skewers, then said, "Kou looked pretty worn-out while the costume team was doing their preparations. Today, he might collapse from all the excitement. I'm not sure the Princesses can handle it alone."

"Oh…? Now that you mention it, Kou, you're not looking too good," murmured Mirei, concern in her voice.

He brought a hand to his cheek. It was true that he hadn't been sleeping that well the past few days. It seemed his fatigue had started showing on his face without his noticing.

Both Princesses nodded in firm agreement with Tsubaki's suggestions.

"That's a wonderful idea, Tsubaki. I was also concerned about Kou. It would be incredibly encouraging to have everyone with us," said White Princess.

"I agree," added Black Princess. "I wouldn't be able to do anything if it came down to it… I would appreciate your help."

Everyone's eyes gathered on Kou. It seemed they were waiting on his response.

He worried over what to do.

Shouldn't they go their separate ways, like they had the last two times? There was no guarantee they wouldn't run into Asagiri or Isumi despite the chaos of the festival.

Even so, Kou nodded slowly and said, "If everyone is happy doing that, then I'd love to."

Through his experience repeating time over and over, Kou had come to learn something: Interpersonal relationships were incredibly precious.

He didn't want to make light of everyone's kindness.

And if it came down to it, he could just go back in time.

He pretended not to notice how dismissive he was being of a dangerous situation.

* * *

Tsubaki declared that "the true purpose of a festival was to buy and eat."

Hikami questioned her logic, but his counterargument was rejected.

In accordance with Tsubaki's declaration, the first thing Mirei, Hikami, Tsubaki, Kou, and the Princesses did was buy candy.

The candy they bought was kind of lottery lollipop. If you happened to get the special kind, the lollipop stick would change shape once you were finished eating.

Tsubaki, Hikami, Kou, and White Princess had normal sticks, but a crystal rose appeared on the tip of Mirei's, and a butterfly grew on the tip of Black Princess's.

Hikami appeared impressed. "That's incredible. It looks like they prepped the crystals with magic and did some calculations so they'd rapidly morph when exposed to air... Your average student would have to put in a lot of study to pull off something like that."

"Don't be ridiculous, Hikami. You're not supposed to analyze it, just admire its beauty," said Mirei with a smile.

Hikami made a face.

Black Princess hesitantly stroked a wing of the butterfly. White Princess smiled, happy for her.

Next, the six of them went to buy some drinks made by the Department of Magic Research.

These, too, had a sort of novelty to them. They all looked exactly the same, but if you got an unlucky one, it would rapidly react once exposed to air and become incredibly spicy.

Hikami was the lucky one here, writhing in silent agony. He took a drink of water offered by Mirei, then angrily declared, "I need to make a complaint about these. That's so spicy it'll be no laughing matter if a student with a low tolerance gets hit with one."

He continued, insisting they should protest the drinks. He wasn't concerned for himself, he said; he was just angry over the slight chance of someone else being harmed. Everyone tried calming him down.

"Relax, Hikami. This sort of thing is part of the fun of festivals. Just think of it as getting run over by a Type A kihei."

"Which would immediately kill me, right, Mirei?"

"Yeah, it probably would."

The topic seemed a little inappropriate for a joke.

Black Princess tentatively touched her tongue to her drink, then looked relieved.

They all sipped their drinks as they walked. At one point, Tsubaki tugged on Hikami's hair.

"Oh? I see something over there. Stop, Hikami."

"I think it might be time for you to get down soon, Tsubaki," he replied.

There was a magic show in the middle of the road. The performers were street performers from the capital.

They performed a trick where they sawed the body of one of the performers in half, and Tsubaki and Mirei gasped in admiration. At that point, it looked like Hikami had figured out a few of their tricks, but he could tell the others were enjoying themselves and kept it to himself.

Black Princess was the only person to let out a real scream. She shook Kou's shoulder in a panic and said, "I—I could survive that, but a normal human would die!"

"Black Princess," said Kou, "it's just a trick. It's okay. They won't die."

"He's right, Black Princess. You don't have to worry," said White Princess, and the two of them managed to calm Black Princess down. Her mouth was still agape, but she listened to them and nodded. The performers looked happy to get such an honest response from a member of the audience.

Kou and the others tossed some money in a hat placed on the ground, then left.

As they walked, Tsubaki, the Princesses, and Hikami bought some cotton candy. The candy looked like massive clouds.

All of them except Hikami went to town on the candy.

"There's so much. But I'm not going to lose!" said Tsubaki.

"Black Princess and I will pull off an exquisite win," said White Princess.

"Was eating candy a kind of sport…?" asked Black Princess.

Hikami, on the other hand, was pulling off the cotton candy bit by bit and passing it to *something*. The candy disappeared into thin air. Apparently Hikami had brought Unknown along with them, and they just couldn't see her. Now that Kou thought about it, he realized Hikami had been sharing all his delicious food for a while now.

The six of them walked on, looking for more stalls as they battled over sweet candy.

* * *

Eventually, they came to the edge of the area with the stalls. That's when something happened.

Tsubaki, still on Hikami's shoulders, called out, "Look, Sasanoe's running."

"Hmm? Oh, you're right; that's Sasanoe," said White Princess as she craned her neck and shaded her eyes with her hand.

With Crimson Princess in tow, he was threading through the crowd so swiftly it almost seemed like magic. Kagura chased after him. It seemed it really was Sasanoe's fate to be dragged to the haunted house.

But then, once again, there was a change.

"…Huh, you guys," said Sasanoe as he noticed the six of them. He kicked off the ground, rushed around a corner, and quickly closed the remaining distance, stopping at the last possible moment before crashing into them. He then handed *something* over to them.

"Take care of her," he said.

"Huh? Sasanoe, uh… You want us to take Crimson Princess?" asked Kou as Sasanoe set her down between Kou's Princesses with a thud.

It seemed like he wanted to spare her. But at the same time, White Princess and Crimson Princess didn't get along that well, and Crimson Princess didn't look like she wanted to leave Sasanoe. She frowned and narrowed her crimson eyes.

An odd tension passed between the three Brides.

And then…

"Here you are! I finally found you."

"Huh?" said Kou as he felt a tug at his arm.

He turned to see a female student with vibrant honey-colored hair. She clung close to Kou as if they knew each other well. She was staring up at him, her beautiful features peeking out from behind her owl mask.

"I've been looking for you, dear," she said cheerfully. "Come on, let's go."

"Uh, I'm—"

"Sorry, please play along," she whispered.

Kou followed her glance to two large male students. It looked like there was something going on among them and that she was looking for a way to escape.

"Okay, let's go," she said. "I'm so glad I found you." She tugged on his arm and tried to move away.

Kou looked back at the rest of the group. They were all focused on Crimson Princess. Black Princess tried to stroke her crimson hair, only to have her hand bitten without warning. It would be easy for him to call out to them from here.

But if this is all a coincidence, and she honestly needs help, then all I have to do is go with her for a second. And if not…then I can't just let her get away.

If this was another part of whatever was going on, he couldn't let it go.

He decided to go with the girl.

He let her guide him back into the clamor of the festival.

* * *

"You've realized something's off, haven't you? And yet you still came with me... That's incredible," said the girl, an odd singsong rhythm to her words.

She pulled off her owl mask with a dance-like flourish. Eyes the same color as her honeyed hair stared at Kou. Just as he'd expected, she had a beautiful face. Those defined features would surely attract many of the male students. She winked.

Then she tossed something toward Kou.

It was a sword with a blunted blade.

As long as you were careful, you could stab or cut at someone with it and still avoid causing any major damage.

Kou caught the sword. "What are you doing?" he asked.

"There's no need to be unfriendly. My name's Helze Kakitsubata. You can call me Helze."

Helze grinned wide and bowed deeply.

There was a cheer from the crowd around them.

Kou and Helze were inside a ringed stage for fighting.

Around the ring were chairs for spectators. Besides those, there were no other decorations to get in the way of the fight. This place was normally used by the Department of Combat for practice. Now they were inviting participants for another festival event.

The event itself was both glamorous and unsettling—a series of public duels.

People placed bets were on each round, and the winner took a small part of the earnings. Thus, it was a gathering spot for those with confidence in their abilities. This was an event suited to the Academy, since the students here were soldiers as well, and the teachers had officially approved it.

And this was where Helze had led Kou.

She filled out his application, then dragged him, confused, into the ring.

Now, with swords in hand, they faced off.

"The match is decided when either side lands a strike with their sword," cried the fourth-year student acting as referee. "Ready, set... Go!" They brought their arm down sharply.

Helze twirled the sword in her hand. Kou raised his guard, though he didn't have any intention of fighting her.

He didn't know what she wanted. He had just decided he would throw the fight when things took a sudden turn.

Helze rushed across the ground on her slender legs with explosive speed. "...Ah!"

Kou reflexively brought his sword up in front of his face to guard.

Metal clashed against metal.

The audience cheered.

Onlookers could keep placing bets for the first few minutes of the match. It seemed like a lot of people were now betting on Helze. The numbers displayed on the wall were changing so quickly it was enough to make your head spin. There were shouts of encouragement and jeers from the crowd, hounding Helze to finish him off and telling Kou not to give up yet.

They were all so carefree, Kou thought bitterly.

The audience hadn't realized. Neither had the referee. Only Kou could see it.

That last attack had been aimed directly at Kou's eyes.

I don't think she's going to let me throw this fight.

Kou steeled himself. He leaped backward, putting distance between Helze and him.

Helze hummed a tune and swayed from side to side as she stroked her sword seductively.

As if continuing the song, she whispered, "I'm generally not in charge of the big, rough boys like this one. I'm a fan of the smaller, good boys. I'll make sure to show you next time. I hope you'll look forward to it."

"Could you please stop joking around? Who are you? And what are you up to?"

"Who am I? Such a simple question, but it cuts right to the heart of the matter."

She moved again, gazing vaguely toward the sky. With her right leg planted on the ground, her left leg lashed out in a kick.

Kou crouched down to evade, letting the sharp strike pass over his head. Even as she attacked, Helze continued speaking, her tone relaxed. "Who am I? Hmm…yes…"

Unlike her words, her attacks were so powerful they would likely do more than just knock her opponent unconscious. Helze bent forward as she followed up with a jab of her sword. Kou stepped to the left, slipping by the haphazard strike.

In an instant, she had stepped in close, swinging a powerful punch. Kou leaped back to dodge.

The crowd cheered louder.

They threw ribbons into the air, perhaps in appreciation of the dance-like movements.

But what was happening in front of them was a real fight to the death.

And no one seemed to notice.

"…Have you heard of the Puppets, Mr. Pandemonium?"

"The Puppets…?"

Kou repeated Helze's words, and as he did so, he remembered something he had heard before.

* * *

The warning he had received from Shuu Hibiya:

"There are others besides me who have returned from the imperial capital. I imagine you're destined to meet them. But running into them at night in Central Headquarters would put you at a distinct disadvantage."

"Are they the ones back from the imperial capital?" asked Kou.

"Oh, so you've heard of us? Yes. Usually, we remain in the capital to guard important people. We are the 'nonexistent' class zero of the Department of Combat, a special squad made only from the most powerful students—those capable of killing kihei even without magic armor."

They were called the Puppets.

Kou gasped at Helze's smooth explanation.

What she was describing differed significantly from the capabilities of regular Department of Combat students who had to wear magic armor.

He'd never heard of anyone who could kill a kihei without it, outside of Pandemonium.

But before anything else, Kou needed to ask a very basic question.

"What do the Puppets want with me?"

"Nothing big, really. We just want you to hand over White Princess."

"No," replied Kou immediately.

Helze smirked. The expression reminded Kou of a cat.

"You won't even ask why? Wonderful. I like that," she said.

"I don't care what you like. I will never hand over White Princess."

"Oh, at least hear me out. It's not like we want to hurt her."

Helze swung down her sword as she spoke. The strike could have cracked Kou's skull.

This girl's words and actions were in complete opposition.

As she continued to speak, her lethal attacks showed no signs of letting up.

"*Various things have changed* because you all survived the Gloaming. There are others who bear you more hostility than us. We Puppets are practically warm and welcoming compared to them. The first thing we want to do is to look for a peaceful resolution. As for this, well, it's my personal hobby."

"Sounds like you have horrible taste," said Kou. "...I have a few more questions for you, but first—" He moved quickly, jumping to the side to dodge her most recent attack.

Through his fifteen thousand repetitions, he had gained massive amounts of fighting experience. He'd already gauged his opponent's sword skills.

Looks like she was telling the truth about being unused to longer swords.

There was a gap between her true ability, which he could glimpse now and again, and the power of her actual attacks. Her motions were a bit stiff, as if she was trying to limit the opening she left after swinging her weapon. That was where Kou struck.

In that brief moment of stillness, he swung his sword.

But she dodged.

He'd expected this.

He immediately threw his sword.

Running at the same speed as the flying sword, he dashed toward Helze and swung his fist.

She danced out of the way of the two attacks. But her evasive maneuvers had put her arm in the exact position Kou had expected. He kicked at the hand holding her sword.

It flew into the air.

He caught it and pressed the blade against her throat.

Her honey-colored eyes narrowed. "A blunt sword won't cut anyone, you know," she murmured in amusement.

"I'll crush your vocal cords if you try to keep fighting," said Kou. "Back down for now... We'll talk again."

"How clever you are. All right. Next time, let's go on a nice, long date." She winked at him, then raised her hands to signal her defeat.

"And the winner is...Kou Kaguro!" declared the referee.

There were groans from those who'd bet on Helze, along with a few cheers from the other side.

Flower petals exploded into the ring.

And so Kou managed to survive his first encounter with the Puppets.

* * *

The moment the fight ended, Helze disappeared like a gust of wind. Kou took his winnings and left.

Sunset had dyed the sky, and he could hear music in the distance. He walked on tired legs. Looking up, he saw crowds of people lining the streets.

The Music Corps was starting another parade in the square. This time, the magic over the bricks wasn't rainbow, but like sparkling stars. This performance seemed to be marking the end of the festival. The music was gentle and elegant.

Ah... The festival's ending soon.

It looked like he would survive this time. He let out a sigh.

And then it happened.

He saw a white figure tottering around. He narrowed his eyes and stared, wondering what it was. It looked like a child walking around with a sheet over their head. Kou guessed it was a little girl, based on the child's build.

She appeared to be a visitor from the imperial capital who was wearing a costume instead of a mask.

Assuming that was the case, he called out to her. "Are you lost? Where's your mommy and daddy?"

"......Mister, are you an ally of justice?" replied the girl, surprising Kou. He blinked. *What was she talking about?* But he didn't want to frighten her.

In as calm a tone as he could muster, he replied, "Yes. I'd like to be."

"Really....? That's......nice," she whispered, sounding moved.

Kou tried to take her hand, but she softly pulled her white palm away. With a wave, she murmured, "Sorry... I could only slip out for a bit... Bye-bye."

"Oh, okay. As long as you're fine on your own."

He watched the girl walk away. She kept waving for some time, but eventually her form was swallowed up into the crowd.

Standing still for a moment, Kou thought back to what had happened earlier.

The Puppets, huh... I'll need to talk to Helze again.

"Koooooooooooou!"

"White Princess, it's dangerous to run at full speed!"

Just as Kou was falling deep into thought, a white mass came flying at him, followed by a shout from Mirei.

It crashed into him with such force that he was nearly knocked backward. But a pair of slender arms grabbed him and held him fast.

White Princess squeezed him tight. "Where did you go, Kou? I was so worried!" She sounded upset.

"Sorry, White Princess... Something suddenly came up. Well, more like it appeared out of nowhere."

"What were you doing? Festivals don't happen every day, you know. I can't believe you left your Brides behind," said Yaguruma.

"...Sorry," said Kou. "But, Yaguruma, it looks like you managed to undo the brainwashing."

"Just about... Wait. How'd you know about that?"

Yaguruma, having finished his turn as the monster and rejoined the group, furrowed his brow. The dangerous glint in his eyes that Kou had noticed when taking the costume last time was gone. Yaguruma tugged at the cloth covering his mouth, looking tired.

Black Princess popped out from behind Yaguruma and hurried to Kou's side. Then she grabbed onto the cuff of his uniform.

"Sorry for worrying you, too, Black Princess," he said.

"Mm… I did worry."

Then the cheers grew louder. It sounded like the parade was reaching its finale. Hundreds of gold feathers danced through the air. They glittered as they passed before Kou's eyes. After finishing their final performance, the Music Corps took a bow.

The sound of applause faded.

The festival was over.

That's when it happened.

He felt a burning sensation in his abdomen.

Kou Kaguro opened his violet eyes.

He looked down at his chest.

The hilt of a knife protruded from his uniform. The long blade was embedded completely in his chest. It was lucky it hadn't directly pierced his heart.

Intense pain struck him, and he knew.

He'd been stabbed.

He slowly looked up and asked the person in front of him:

"…Why?"

There was no response. Yaguruma just looked at him, expressionless.

White Princess screamed something, and Black Princess appeared to be speaking, too.

Tsubaki and Hikami were rushing over.

Kou coughed up blood and felt a hollow laugh well up in his throat.

Something was very odd about this.

Yaguruma pulled the blade from Kou's chest.

The amount of dark-red blood splattering on the ground was almost comical.

His vision wavered from the loss of blood.

The scenery of the Academy around him shook and swam.

His body leaned forward, and he collapsed.

He was dying.

In that moment, he concentrated and closed his eyes, then opened them.

* * *

He traveled back in time.

Kou Kaguro opened his violet eyes.

He was standing in his classroom at twilight—just another normal scene in his life. But there was a reason he had chosen to fly to that point in time. Right now, there was no one but him in the classroom.

The perfect chance to speak with *him*.

He may not have enough information to rely on other people, but he didn't mind involving *himself*.

Kou turned toward the lectern. Behind it stood a man in military uniform, wearing a worn coat.

Kou then asked a question of his other self, Kagura:

"...So what is this all about?"
"Something's happening, right?"

Kagura whispered his reply, with a gaze like he could see through everything and a small smile playing on his lips.

The Bride of Demise

9. THE RESULT OF SURVIVAL

What in the world was happening?

Kou had been through three festivals, and he told Kagura what had happened at all of them.

The teacher stroked his chin as he listened intently to Kou's story. They were all alone in the classroom.

"I see... So that's what's been going on." He hadn't shown much sympathy, even when Kou spoke about dying. His expression unchanging, Kagura held up two fingers and said, "If it were only Asagiri and Isumi, we couldn't entirely rule out the possibility that it was motivated by revenge. You'd be surprised how little it takes to push someone to kill another... But it's definitely unexpected for Yaguruma to stab you. He's not the kind of kid to suddenly harm someone."

"The same goes for Asagiri and Isumi," argued Kou.

"Well, I don't knooow," drawled Kagura. "I mean, I am you. But my memories of them are from so long ago I just don't knooow." Despite his playful tone, he began to seriously consider the problem.

He stroked his face, deep in thought. "To begin with," he murmured. "It's not that odd for someone in Pandemonium to have a weapon when they're going out without their Bride. But why would regular students bring knives to the festival?"

Kou's jaw dropped in realization. Kagura had a point. It was only by chance that he'd run into Asagiri and Isumi. There was no way they would both have reason to carry around a knife just in case.

Kagura crossed his legs where he sat atop the lectern.

"I can think of two possible reasons," he began. "First, your meetings weren't by chance. Or second, all regular students are now required to carry a bare minimum of arms, and the change occurred without my knowledge… The latter would imply a serious intent at work. An intent to kill you, Kou Kaguro."

"Which means Asagiri and Isumi—"

"Were being controlled in order to kill you. Someone is choosing the person nearest to you when the festival ends… Considering how unnatural Yaguruma's action was, this possibility seems quite high. It's a good thing he didn't kill you immediately, but it makes me think whoever's manipulating them doesn't have very fine control."

Kou's hands clenched into fists as he listened.

He'd survived the Gloaming along with all his friends. And yet he still had to die? He didn't understand. It was absurd. But there was no time to cry over it.

There was definitely something strange happening.

There was something Kou had noticed. "One of the Puppets, Helze, said that things had changed because we survived the Gloaming. She also said there were others who were more hostile toward Pandemonium, toward White Princess and me. I was wondering if that might have something to do with it."

"The Puppets? Wow! That's a name I haven't heard in forever. There was a time when Pandemonium got into a huge fight with the then leader of the Puppets. I had heard they were sent to be guards in the imperial capital, but they're back now, huh? That must mean the higher-ups see us surviving the Gloaming as a pretty big deal… Guess that makes sense."

"You said before that the Gloaming was probably caused by humans."

Those words had implied new fights to come.

Kou sucked in a deep breath, then released it. Steeling himself, he asked, "Is there a chance this is related?"

"It's not impossible. That's all I know at the moment," replied Kagura in a low voice. He stretched out his back with a groan, and his joints made unpleasant crackling and popping sounds. With a mix of emotions on his face, he said, "All I know so far is that it's a possibility. I haven't been able to confirm anything since I arrived in this time line and became a teacher. But I have the 'key' I need to confirm it… That's why I intentionally brought Millennium Black Princess to the Academy… It wasn't just a whim, you know?"

"That's why you brought Black Princess here?" asked Kou, not understanding the implication. He frowned, but Kagura just shook his head before continuing on a completely different topic.

"Shuu Hibiya scolded you, right? You're too relaxed. You haven't yet gotten a grip on your power. To you, it's nothing more than infinite free do-overs. If you keep it up and things go south, and if knowledge of your ability gets out, you're going to be in serious trouble. I can't talk much about it yet… But the current problem is what to do about the day of the festival."

Kagura stroked his chin again and thought for a moment.

Before long, he clapped his hands together.

"Go down into the ruins."

* * *

Kagura's guess was this: Someone who wanted Kou dead was using some means to control the students. The control was limited, seeing as they weren't able to make Kou commit suicide, and there seemed to be restrictions on the area of effect, both physically and in terms of timing. If Kou could avoid the surprise attack at the festival even once, then they could easily trace the magic residue back to its source.

The first step was to survive.

Kou and Kagura had decided the most effective strategy would be to hide out in the central labyrinth. And there was another benefit to this choice.

In anticipation of that benefit, Kou took the Princesses with him into the ruins.

"Sorry to make you miss the festival," he said.

"What are you talking about, Kou?" said White Princess. "There's nothing in the world more important than your life. I wish you had spoken with us sooner. The thought of you being stabbed on three occasions infuriates me."

"…A method for manipulating people…," murmured Black Princess. "I can think of several ways, but all of them are horrible. First things first, you need to survive."

The two gladly gave up on going to the festival to accompany Kou.

Special and Type A kihei appeared along their path, but not even a Special Type was a match for White Princess if it appeared alone. She spread her mechanical wings and emitted a blue light.

"You're in the way."

All that remained were the scattered pieces of the defeated kihei.

After tearing down the obstructions in their path, the three of them continued in silence.

Inside the ruins, it was dark, but there were walls that gave off light at regular intervals. As usual, Kou didn't know what they were made from.

They walked on, without needing a light. There was a specific location they were headed.

Eventually, more of their surroundings came into view.

Black birds took to the air. The light of the sun was visible here. Kou looked up to see an open shaft through all seven floors above them and leading to the surface. That was likely why there were so many plants growing there. The ground around them was coated in green. There was even a set of stairs running up along the wall, though it was half collapsed.

Hundreds of birds made their nests on the rubble, and black feathers floated gently to the ground.

This had been the site of their battle with over a hundred kihei.

Once they had arrived, Kou spoke. "All right… I know you've been following us. Let's talk."

Signaled by his voice, several figures appeared behind him.

They weren't kihei; they were human.

It was the Department of Combat's most powerful squad, the 'nonexistent' class zero.

The Puppets.

They'd been waiting for their moment to appear before Kou and the Princesses.

* * *

This was the other benefit.

Helze hadn't approached Kou during his first or second time through the festival. That was probably to avoid a fight with White Princess in the middle of the crowded festival. During the third run, she had determined she could pull Kou away alone and called out to him.

In that case, what would she do if they moved into the ruins?

The three of them leaving the festival was obviously abnormal, and the Puppets would surely have something to say about it.

Kou had guessed as much, and he was right. They had planned to make contact.

This would allow Kou to ask the Puppets some questions.

The girl with honey-colored hair was the first to step forward.

"Nice to meet you. My name is Helze. Helze Kakitsubata. It's a pleasure to make your acquaintance."

She bowed gracefully.

Helze and Kou hadn't met yet, not *this time*.

She brushed back her honey-colored hair, acting like this was their first meeting. Kou nodded once and looked at the others. Most of them were wearing the regular Academy military uniform, except that it was navy, and their faces were hidden under hoods.

Their identities remained unclear.

Nonetheless, it was easy to tell from their physiques that they were all familiar with combat.

One of them looked at Kou and murmured, "How curious... His build isn't that impressive, yet his eyes are those of a great warrior with countless battles under his belt..."

"He's a different sort than Sasanoe, but this should still be fun," said another, giggling. "The students of Pandemonium are our only real opponents."

Helze, too, smiled at Kou.

But her facade of friendliness quickly melted away. "We are the Puppets, and we have a request."

"I refuse to hand over White Princess," replied Kou. "But I do have a few questions I want answered."

"Oh my, our target has been leaked? And you want to talk to me?" asked Helze, though she didn't seem particularly upset. Kou nodded.

Beside him stood White Princess, her blue eyes narrowed. She asked him wordlessly if these people were their enemies.

Kou gestured with his hand for her to hold back. "It seems various things have changed because we survived the Gloaming. I've heard there are others who bear us—White Princess and me, perhaps even Pandemonium—more hostility than you. I'd like you to tell me about them."

"Hmm, you understand the danger of your situation better than I thought... But for you to know so much must mean... Puppets, have any of you talked?"

Helze suddenly addressed the others behind her, though the one who had spoken with Kou was none other than herself. However, one person did hesitantly raise their hand. It was a girl, her hair done in twin braids. She seemed hesitant.

"Um, I think we might have been overheard when we were talking in the café."

"Oh dear. Nina, you really do like to talk. Oh well. Now about this other power." Helze clapped her hands together as her honey-colored eyes sparkled. She sounded truly happy as she spoke. "If you don't change your ways...you're going to die."

"...Why do I have to die?"

"That's right; it's so unfair it makes no sense." Helze nodded sympathetically but then continued smoothly. "You did such a wonderful job ending the Gloaming. And *that's* why... Right from the start, there were many people opposed to Pandemonium getting ahold of the seventh member of the Princess Series. The problem is, you can't change a Bride's mind once they've chosen their Groom, and they're difficult to destroy... Most importantly, Kagura forced through an agreement. When that man really wants something, he can pretty much get it."

Kou's eyes narrowed at the mention of Kagura. This sounded odd. He couldn't believe Kagura was that skilled at negotiating.

Helze noticed Kou's doubtful expression and continued her explanation.

"If Kagura wanted, he could *destroy the balance of the world*. He has the power to do whatever he wants. It's a miracle they're able to keep him in line at all. That's why you were able to keep your Princess...and how you managed to survive the Gloaming. With Pandemonium having lost almost no one in battle, class one hundred has gained unprecedented power... They have Sasanoe, Shirai, Yurie, and...you, Kou Kaguro. The situation isn't what I'd call favorable."

"...Why?"

"You don't get it? Even though Kagura can destroy the balance of the world, he can't take control of the country. The world would be destroyed if he used too much of his power. But...as the leader of the current Pandemonium, he could potentially take the imperial capital. Therefore, we have a need to pare down its membership."

Kou was struck with a realization, and at the same time, he began to feel dizzy.

It was all just so...trivial.

"So you need to kill the one who kept casualties low due to some hypothetical threat?" asked Kou.

"Exactly. And we're supposed to disguise it as someone's isolated act." Helze smiled.

Kou thought back to his three times through the festival. In each of those instances, he'd been stabbed by a single person.

Helze scowled as she continued. "I'll tell you a little about the method. It's meant to prevent White Princess from becoming hostile toward the general public or to the forces at work. Afterward, they'll take in a portion of Pandemonium along with White Princess, now masterless, and change their affiliation... That's what they have in mind anyway."

"It won't work. Even if Kou dies, I will do everything to bring him back," said White Princess. Her glossy hair was standing on end in anger, rising slightly from her scalp.

Kou knew that the result of White Princess trying to overcome Kou's death was Black Princess, who stood behind him. But Helze didn't know about White Princess's ability.

She gave a little shrug. "So you'd overcome death itself. How passionate! To be honest, I think the plan to kill you and take in White Princess is as sloppy as it gets, but they don't seem to understand that... Those people just want to weaken Pandemonium; they don't care about anything else. It's incredibly dangerous. Which is why I was hoping to negotiate."

"Your plan's sloppy, too...," said Kou. "Sorry, but there's no way a Groom would hand over their Bride."

"Of course. Which is why I have another proposal," said Helze. "Kou Kaguro, would you consider joining the Puppets?" She spread out her arms in invitation.

She looked as innocent as a child inviting someone to come play.

Kou frowned. As he watched, Helze spun around pointlessly.

Her invitation didn't end there. In a singsong voice, she continued. "In this short time, I've really come to like you. You might even call it love. We Puppets are a close bunch. I can guarantee you'll enjoy being with us. We can even protect you from unnecessary meddling if you join. What do you think? I sincerely suggest you take me up on this."

Kou was silent for a few moments. He couldn't figure out Helze or any of the other Puppets. But he could tell one thing for certain: Her proposal came from a place of honest goodwill.

Which is why he gave an honest, straightforward response.

"I'm sorry, I can't do that. I have a lot of friends in Pandemonium."

"Awww. That's too bad. Guess you can't throw away your friends that easily. I get that. Now, then."

Helze instantly twitched. Kou nodded and looked at White Princess. She spread her mechanical winds.

There was the sharp sound of metal on metal as White Princess repelled a small blade that had flown toward Kou.

Helze's smile didn't falter as she said, "Our only choice now is to fight to the death."

"What will you do about White Princess once you've killed me?" asked Kou.

"We'll do our best to chase her down until she's no longer operational, then recover her."

"You're pretty confident."

"Well, orders are orders; all we can do is follow them. We're underlings, after all."

The other Puppets started moving.

Only Kou and White Princess stood against them. Though they also had Black Princess, they couldn't let the Puppets find out about her real power. Anyone who discovered she was Millennium Black Princess would have to die.

"Black Princess, fall back; it's dangerous."

"Kou… If I fight…We'll almost certainly win. But…I can't, can I?"

"No, you can't. You stay there. White Princess?"

"Yes, Kou. I give you my control, my servitude, my trust…"

Her blue eyes shone. Kou could see from her beautiful profile how resolved she was to fight as she whispered.

"This I swear, Kou: I will kill everything that stands in your way."

And so the battle began.

The Puppets versus Pandemonium's Phantom Rank.

* * *

"Kou!"

"Yes, White Princess."

She plucked a feather from her mechanical wings. Kou accepted it and slashed at Helze, but his strike was knocked off course by a sharp cut from the side. Kou's eyes widened. His current opponent wielded an unusual weapon.

Its blade was long and thin. If you swung with all your might, it might break. It was a katana.

A slender male student held the sword. In a low voice, he whispered, "The name's Touji Kurumada. I'm honored to fight a Phantom Rank from Pandemonium."

"You're so annoying, Touji! Get out of the way!" came a girl's voice, accompanied by hundreds of metal bullets.

White Princess spread her mechanical wings and stopped them all, though several left dents.

She blinked at that. "Oh, that's a lot of power. It surprised me."

"I know, right!" replied the girl, sounding proud.

She was the one from before—the girl with twin braids named Nina.

Kou was surprised, too. Guns weren't normally used in fights against kihei. In order to take down a kihei with a gunshot, it had to have enough force to pierce through their armor. And you had to burn through bullets to do it.

Most kihei in the ruins would require more bullets than you could possibly stock.

Trying to use magic to create bullets from the materials in the ground had its own problems. You could get more power with far less waste by simply applying direction and emitting power from magic armor.

But, Kou thought bitterly, *guns are more than effective at killing humans.*

"Hey, you, I bet you were just thinking 'guns are more than effective at killing humans,' right?" This was Nina again, her hands poised on her slender hips. The other Puppets were holding back, perhaps out of consideration for her. It seems they were as close as Helze had said.

Nina patted her machine gun and puffed out her small chest with pride. "Too bad for you! I get by against kihei with just one of these bad boys! Guns have a lot of potential. They could allow even regular students to have a chance against the kihei. I'm proof of that."

"Yes, yes, Nina. Are you done?" said Helze as she stepped forward, almost dancing.

Kou increased his guard, but she had already found an opening and came swooping toward his chest. The movement was natural, like a girlfriend leaning in to give her boyfriend a kiss. Kou immediately fell backward.

A small blade caressed the space where his throat had been.

From his leaning position, he swung his sword horizontally. That deflected Touji's katana, putting some space between them.

Just then, Nina's gun roared, but White Princess opened her wings. "I won't let you," she said. "Kou is my beloved." She stopped every single bullet, while shooting a blue light in Touji's direction.

A moment earlier, he had slipped his katana back into its sheath. Then he drew the blade and slashed in one fluid motion.

"Hiyah!"

And sliced the light.

It was absurd, illogical.

But Kou didn't have time to say anything.

Helze had hurled a spray of countless needles at him.

He rolled to the side, noticing that all of them had poison applied to the tip. As he tried to stand, he felt a shiver run down his spine. He leaped forward on instinct. Someone's fist crunched into the ground he'd just been standing on.

"Barefisted?!" he exclaimed in surprise.

"I'm wearing specially made protective gloves. The end goal is to fight barefisted," replied a girl's voice.

Kou's eyes widened. Before him stood a beautiful girl, the sleeves of her uniform rolled up. Her long hair fluttered as she raised her fists.

With a smile, she introduced herself. "I'm Harusaki Shimanaga. I used to train individually under Shuu Hibiya. I'm excited to have the chance to fight one of Pandemonium's Phantom Ranks, so I hope you'll give it your all."

"You might be excited to fight four against two," said Kou, "but I can't say the same."

"My apologies, but please bear with us. I'd prefer to fight one-on-one myself," said Harusaki with a wry smile. "And we're still only scoping you out, by the way. Please feel free to call us cowards when we come at you ten or more at a time."

From that, Kou inferred that the majority of the Puppets had yet to mobilize. They had a lot of people still in reserve.

They know we don't mean them any harm, thought Kou bitterly, *and they're still doing this…*

Kou had no intention of killing them. Students killing each other was the height of absurdity.

He had no desire to take the life of another person.

By now, he'd gathered all the information he could. His next goal was to put a few of the Puppets out of commission before making his escape.

The Puppets could read his plans, and still they continued, smiling.

Kou would have to learn.

This was just what the Puppets were like.

* * *

After less than a minute of fighting, Kou had figured out each of the Puppets' different roles.

Nina was there to pin down White Princess. Touji was guarding Nina. And Helze and Harusaki were targeting Kou.

Kou knocked aside several small, airborne daggers and evaded a fist. He sighed as he put some distance between himself and his two opponents.

They're strong... Really strong.

Their movements were abnormal. The experience he'd gained through his fifteen thousand repetitions wasn't proving very helpful against them.

Even now, Helze was wobbling around as if drunk. These movements seemed pointless, but when she suddenly unleashed an attack, it was sharp and precise.

It was difficult to predict what direction the next one would come from.

Harusaki's attacks, on the other hand, were always perfect. As supple as a snake, as sharp as a bee, her fists came hunting for his blood.

Kou continued to evade these disparate attack styles using White Princess's vision, but he was kept busy with defense.

Faced with these two opponents, he was having a hard time finding a window to attack.

Harusaki's fist grazed his cheek. Blood spattered, and he lost sight in his left eye.

A poisoned needle flew in from his blind spot, but he knocked it away with the flat of his blade. Helze pouted.

"Come on! Isn't this kind of a special occasion? Go ahead and let one in. You'll be amazed how little it hurts. I can guarantee it; I use these good little boys all the time."

"Whether they hurt really isn't the issue here," replied Kou. "And no, thank you."

Helze laughed, seeming truly pleased.

White Princess, on the other hand, let out a heavy sigh. She was blocking bullets as they came flying toward her and trying to destroy the machine gun with a beam of blue light. Once again, Touji sliced through the light. Its remnants struck the gun but had no effect.

White Princess gazed at the indents in her wings and whispered, "I see... That's some sophisticated magical technology."

"Oh, good eye! We're the ones developing it. Amazing, right?" said Nina proudly. White Princess let out another heavy sigh.

Kou understood. White Princess wanted to blow the Puppets away with no concern for if they lived or died, and she would be able to. He also realized that it was foolish of him to try to spare them, when they were clearly after his life. Not to mention the Puppets would likely die smiling even if Kou did let White Princess kill them. But he couldn't allow things to end like that. There was no logic in students killing each other.

Still stuck defending himself, Kou thought, *There's...got to be some way to distract them.*

"...Yes, that's it," murmured Black Princess from behind Kou. "Only a few children can still hear my voice, but... Come, all of you."

Kou's eyes narrowed at her words.

For a while, nothing happened. But suddenly, Kou felt the presence of something else behind him.

Even Harusaki narrowed her eyes before stepping back.

Helze whistled briefly. "Oh my, how rude of you all," she murmured. "Not that any of you are going to listen..."

Harusaki spoke up at the same time. "Are they butting in? Well, I guess we *are* in the ruins."

Both girls' eyes were locked on a group of oddly formed figures. Numerous Type As and Special Types were coming from the entrance. With legs more powerful than a human's, they ran across the stone walls.

Helze instantly began launching knives. The blades bore into one kihei's joints, and their corrosive poison melted the Type A's arms and legs. Harusaki flew in a clean arc above its head.

"Hiyah!"

Her fist crashed down with all the force of a cannonball. The single strike, cloaked in magic, crushed the Type A's head.

"Let's go!"

Nina began firing at a Special Type. Thousands of bullets struck its surface, turning it into a smoking corpse. But another kihei appeared over the remains of the first.

White Princess kicked off the ground, drawing Kou and Black Princess into her arms. She turned her back, and her mechanical wings glowed gold.

"Hah!"

She slashed one wing at a kihei rushing toward them, turning the newly arrived Type A into scrap metal.

Kou and White Princess were aware that Black Princess had called these kihei, but with her wings concealed, she didn't have very fine control over them.

The kihei were targeting Kou and the Princesses, too.

White Princess started moving as she continued to cut down kihei, trying to get to a place where they could escape from the Puppets. However, they could see several more figures flying down from the vertical shaft. White Princess fired off another round of blue light.

It was starting to turn into a full-blown melee.

"Just cutting down kihei isn't any fun," said Touji as he slashed one in half vertically.

Nina's machine gun brought down multiple kihei in one go.

Kou took White Princess's arm and stepped down to the ground, then slashed the head from a kihei blocking their path.

The other Puppets had begun to engage as well. Dozens of figures scattered out across the area, and the room filled with the sound of slashing and bashing. Metal and organic components tumbled to the ground. Both sides whittled away at the kihei force.

If Kou and the Princesses were going to get away, they had to do so now.

They made an attempt to dash for the exit. Helze started to chase them but suddenly stopped.

"Huh…? What did you just say?" she said as she pressed a hand to her left ear.

Kou unconsciously stopped where he was and waited, his brow furrowed.

There was a communications device in Helze's ear. Unlike the one Kou had given to White Princess, this one was audio only.

Helze's face twisted in confusion.

She clicked her tongue loudly. Her attitude had undergone a complete change as she quietly turned back to Kou. "We're calling it quits for today. The mood's been ruined, even for me. You have my sincerest condolences."

"Wait, what happened?" Kou asked, at a loss.

She shook her head, seeming sincerely pained. After looking down for a moment, she lifted her face and said:

"Several members of Pandemonium have been stabbed by regular students."

Over ten of them had been killed by the sudden, random acts of violence.

*   *   *

Kou felt like he'd been kicked in the head as he came to an immediate realization.

His attacker had been trying to reduce Pandemonium's strength by killing him. But because Kou wasn't available, the plan had failed. So of all things, they had decided to switch targets.

Now the plan was to weaken Pandemonium by attacking them as a whole.

When Kou Kagura lived through the festival, this was the result.

The Bride of Demise

10. THE PHANTOM RANKS' DECISION

"Hey, welcome back. And...sorry. I didn't think the enemy was this idiotic," said Kagura, greeting Kou and the Princesses near the entrance to the Academy.

His one blue and one black eye were slightly narrowed in an icy rage Kou didn't often see in Kagura.

"Should I kill everyone involved in making this decision...?" he continued, voice chilling. "Though, I couldn't keep the world from shifting out of phase if I did that. What would happen to the kids who were able to survive...? That's what I'm currently debating. To think they might have even predicted this dilemma, I'm so pissed off right now."

"What happened to everyone?" asked Kou, nearly out of breath. He wiped the sweat from his brow and looked up.

The festival was over. Confetti and ribbons lay scattered lifelessly across the brick walkways. There weren't any stalls near the entrance, and few people were in the area. But Kou could hear the ruckus continuing in the distance. Somewhere, someone was crying. The air quivered with the sound of people's shouts.

It was more than enough for Kou to tell the festival was still in chaos.

"Tsubaki and Yaguruma are dead," said Kagura bluntly.

Kou's breath caught in his throat. Images of Tsubaki's and Yaguruma's smiles floated through his mind, then faded.

The Princesses, too, were at a loss for words. They squeezed each other's hands. There was something empty about a death with no visible corpse, something even more horrible. It brought a heavy despair that felt endless.

His gaze serious and tone flat, Kagura went. "Hikami's Bride protected him. Since Unknown has the power to disappear, she had accompanied him to the festival. Hikami tried to jump in front of Mirei to protect her, but she still suffered serious injuries... And I'm in no mood to calm anyone's anger right now."

His tone became hushed, as if he was uncertain about something. He cast a glance farther into the Academy.

Instantly Kou dashed off, the Princesses following behind him. They quickly found a crowd of people and pushed their way through.

As he ran, Kou tried to mentally sort out what was happening.

Regular students stabbed members of Pandemonium one after another.

Most of Pandemonium were without their Brides during the festival, and no one had expected they'd be stabbed by their fellow students inside the walls of the Academy. Many were taken by surprise and killed.

But that wasn't all.

The chaos wasn't over yet.

"Excuse me, move aside... Let me through," Kou cried as he pushed the crowd aside and leaped into the square. Once there, he quickly grasped the current situation.

Sasanoe stood in the center of the crowd. By his side, floating in the air, was Crimson Princess.

Her liquid silver wings were spread wide. She had likely brought them out to protect Sasanoe from the various blades aimed at him. But that decision had resulted in a new problem.

The kihei were humanity's enemy, and Brides were a secret. But now, in front of this crowd, their existence had been revealed.

"My apologies, Sasanoe...," said Crimson Princess. "You could have dodged those attacks alone."

"Why apologize? Fool, I am proud of your actions, not ashamed," replied Sasanoe.

Kou glanced around the square. If it had been Crimson Princess alone, they might have been able to find some way out of this situation. But two other kihei were here as well, standing out from the crowd.

"My precious Sister... What should we do? There were some bad boys and girls."

Yurie, a well-mannered girl with black hair, was seated on the ground. Her pale legs were stretched out in front of her, and she was smiling sweetly. Beside her stood her Full Humanoid Bride, Sister.

There was a sharp gleam in Sister's eyes as she fiercely protected Yurie.

"*Sigh*... So it's come to this? Not ideal," said Shirai, standing beside Yurie with his feet planted wide. His Special Type Bride, Nameless, was swirling around him. Nameless's formless, liquid body displayed intense rage.

Kou could guess what was happening. Sasanoe, Yurie, and Shirai were all Phantom Rank. Sasanoe had been with Crimson Princess from the beginning, but Yurie and Shirai's Brides were so incredible that they had probably rushed to their Grooms' side the second they sensed danger.

And now they had been exposed in front of the regular students.

The students had been shouting and screaming for a little while now, and their voices had merged into a buzzing like that of bees' wings, but Kou was finally starting to pick out individual voices and hear what they were saying.

"Kihei!"

"Why...? Why are there kihci in the Academy?"

"Where is Combat? Get armed and go after them!"

Despite the shouts of anger and shrieks of fear washing over him, Sasanoe didn't waver in the slightest. He looked up into the sky and let out a heavy sigh. That's when Kou realized there were several corpses at Sasanoe's feet.

They were the members of Pandemonium who had been stabbed and killed. Some of their bodies had been left lying out.

Kou's hands clenched into tight fists.

"All regular students flee!"

"Kihei have appeared within the Academy. We will eliminate them!"

The throngs of people suddenly parted, revealing a group wearing magic armor. It was the Department of Combat. At this rate, it would be students killing students. Kou began to panic.

All of a sudden, Sasanoe shouted into the sky.

"So this is how you repay us?!"

Everyone stopped, intimidated by the power behind Sasanoe's voice.

Before the echo of his shout faded, he moved to strike his liquid silver sword into the brick walkway.

He began to speak to any enemy who wasn't there. "We fought, and we fell in the Gloaming. We tried to protect the Academy, even when faced with death. We fought because the strong have a duty to protect the weak. And we were proud of that! And *this* is how you repay us? Putting knives in the hands of the weak and plunging them into our guts?"

"Sasanoe...," murmured Kou.

"Fine, then... Crimson Princess, are you with me?"

"As you wish," said Crimson Princess. "Neither fear nor pain nor death can separate us."

Sasanoe nodded and lifted his sword into the sky. The setting sun lit the silver blade like it was on fire. Below its gleam, Sasanoe strung his words together heavily.

"The regular students have rejected us. There is nothing we can do about that. But I cannot allow those involved in this to live. We will get past this and then sink our teeth into their throats... Yurie, Shirai, are you with me?!"

He called on the other two as if it was obvious they'd agree.

Yurie wrung her hands and nodded childishly. Shirai silently raised his fist into the air.

Neither showed any sign of nervousness as they responded.

Everyone was frozen around them. The Combat students stood stock-still, as if listening to a performance.

At the center of the commotion, Sasanoe gave his fatal declaration.

"With the deaths of our companions, we of the Phantom Rank abandon the Academy!"

The Bride of Demise

11. THE WORST POSSIBLE OUTCOME

Kou considered the current situation.

Most likely, Sasanoe's decision was yet another part of the enemy's plan. With this, the Academy would be free to handle Pandemonium's power as they saw fit. But still...

Sasanoe had no other choice.

Kou bit his lip. He knew.

Sasanoe was a proud student. He had both great strength and deep affection for Pandemonium. Because he was so strong, he held the ideal of protecting the weak higher than any other.

And that was precisely why he could never forgive the Academy's decision.

Even knowing it was an underhanded trap laid by the enemy, he was so angry he could do nothing but step right into it.

Kou closed his eyes and considered the outcome.

Just then, he heard a low whisper from somewhere nearby.

"...Even if they're Phantom Ranks, breaking away from the Academy is reckless... But they probably won't stop. Even I couldn't stand against all three. Perhaps Kagura could, but it's clear what side he'd choose."

"Hibiya...?" asked Kou, turning to the side.

Hibiya gazed at Sasanoe and the other two with a pained expression. They took a cigarette from their chest pocket and lit it.

"As things are, we're headed for an all-out war... And we'll probably lose."

"Even if we have Sasanoe, Yurie, Shirai, and Kagura on our side?" asked Kou.

"We can't see any of our opponent's cards. Anyone who thinks they have a shot in that situation has got more than a few screws loose. But you have a third choice, don't you, Kou Kaguro?"

"Me...?"

Hibiya glanced sideways at Kou. They smiled slightly and spoke as the cigarette bobbed in their mouth. "You—or White Princess. Either is fine. I've got an idea of your abilities. Normally, I'd keep you from abusing them, but I won't stop you now. Do as you like... And in return, I want you to deliver a message to me, if we meet."

"I will. What should I say?"

"Tell me 'Turn and peel away the skin.' What we need in this situation isn't me as a teacher."

Hibiya blew out a thin stream of smoke. Kou had no idea what those words meant.

Despite that, he gave a small nod.

This was something only he could do.

With a tragic future unfolding before him, Kou decided it was time to act.

However. Kou glared ahead. His fists were clenched. He was a Phantom Rank, too.

"Take care of Black Princess for me," he said to Hibiya. "I'm going to fight as hard as I can... Before I go back, I need to see as much of our opponent's hand as possible."

"That's good. The greatest use of your power is the ability to glean information. Even if you start over, you'll only flounder without enough intel. Just avoid instant death. That would be the end of everything."

"Understood," replied Kou shortly. He raised his head.

Before his eyes, the fight between the Phantom Ranks and the Department of Combat was about to begin. Crude sets of magic armor moved to their predetermined locations.

As they did so, Crimson Princess turned her wings into a vortex before launching it forward. The attack was just weak enough that it wouldn't destroy the magic armor. The waves caressed the air, sending the Combat students toppling.

Over the sounds of collision, a childish laugh rang out.

"Ah-ha-ha-ha-ha-ha! Heyyy, everybody! It's sleepy time!"

Yurie spread her arms wide, laughing joyously. With each laugh, Sister brandished the steal wires in her hands. Making good use of the Academy's festive decorations, she strung up several suits of magic armor, dangling them in the air.

Shirai didn't even need to move.

He rendered all the Combat students unable to fight without inflicting a single wound.

Sasanoe looked around him and snorted. Murmurs rippled through the crowd of regular students. Unable to flee, they simply stepped aside and let the Phantom Ranks pass through like royalty.

Sasanoe set off toward Central Headquarters.

"Let's go, White Princess," said Kou.

"Of course, Kou. I will remain by your side."

He took her hand and dashed off. The crowd was descending into chaos, but no one tried to stop them. Falling into step beside Sasanoe, Kou called out to him, "Sasanoe! As a fellow Phantom Rank, I, Kou Kaguro, and White Princess stand with you."

"You're late, Kou. Come," replied Sasanoe as if he had expected this. He didn't even bother to look in Kou's direction.

Just then, there was a change in the sky above Central Headquarters. Everyone's vision warped violently. The building in front of them, spread out on each side like a great pair of wings, contorted and shifted.

Kou's eyes narrowed. Something was changing. Something ominous was making itself known.

Kou heard someone shouting.

"If they're using that, they must have the principal's approval!"

Kou turned toward the voice, and his eyes widened in surprise.

Had they come running from the ruins? Behind Kou stood Helze and the other Puppets. Only half visible in the gloom, they were staring at the strange sight unfolding in front of them.

At the same time, the oddity appeared—right in front of Central Headquarters.

* * *

It was *something*—but what, Kou didn't know.

A cloth with thick, embroidered magic symbols hung from its head, concealing it. Wings like an owl's poked out from under the cloth on either side. Glowing veins emitted a blue light in the gloom. It was impossible to make out its full countenance.

Kou stared up at the sinister form, eyes narrowed. *What the hell is that...?*

A person's voice rang out, as if a broadcasting device were attached to the *something*.

"Pandemonium has split from the Academy. They have left us no choice. We must take drastic measures."

"But—!"

"If you oppose, does that mean you can stop them before we make our move?" asked the voice. "Well, Puppets?"

Helze hesitated.

She looked down. After a few moments, her attitude seemed to shift. Her gorgeous features turned toward Kou and the others. She raised her arm and leveled it at the Phantom Ranks. Her eyes never left them as she made her declaration.

"We are the Puppets. We have no pride, only power. We will eliminate you."

On her signal, the Puppets scattered into the darkness. It seemed they'd decided their mission based on the voice's provocation.

Countless weapons turned on the Phantom Ranks. Bullets tore through the air. In between bursts of gunfire, daggers flew.

The Puppets' attacks were precise and aimed only at the Grooms. Their brides brushed the projectiles aside.

Normally, someone in the Phantom Rank would be able to wipe the floor with such an opponent. Sasanoe narrowed his eyes.

"I see... So that's your game."

"Yes. This is our true fighting style. I do apologize."

The Puppets were aiming their attacks at Pandemonium from in between the throngs of regular students. If Kou and the others made a careless counterattack, it could harm an innocent bystander.

Whether they had noticed the battle break out or were simply frightened by the kihei, many of the students were trying to flee, but they weren't able to leave. A large number of Puppets had moved to prevent them.

Kou and the others were showered by so many attacks that they didn't even have time to call out the Puppets' cowardly tactics. There were no breaks in their moves.

"Hah!"

Harusaki flew like an arrow from the crowd. Kou hurriedly stepped back. Her fist gouged into the paving slab, before she quickly slipped back into the crowd.

Kou gulped. One wrong step and his heart would be gouged out.

"Aaah!"

Yurie let out a surprised shriek.

Kou glanced over to see an unfamiliar male Puppet aiming a magic weapon at her. Sister swiped it away just before it could fire. Using her steel wires, she skillfully managed to hang several Puppets in the air.

Of those, however, three managed to escape.

A flurry of tiny daggers flew from behind her, but Nameless swallowed them all.

"Hmph!"

Then Touji stepped in, slashing. His attack was aimed at Shirai, but Nameless moved in and took the strike in his stomach. The cut in Nameless's body immediately fused back together.

As it did, Touji escaped into the crowd.

Shirai crossed his arms angrily. "What do we do, Sasanoe?" he muttered. "They can't kill us that easily, but we won't get anywhere at this rate. And then there's that thing." Shirai gestured with his chin toward the strange form still hanging in the air. He knitted his brows and continued, "I don't like the look of it. My Bride agrees, and Nameless is as mysterious as they come... In other words, we don't have a clue what it is. It's not smart to fight something you don't understand, since you've got no idea what it'll throw at you."

"But that *thing* itself must be the most powerful assassin they've sent after us. Can we move forward without defeating it?" asked Sasanoe.

"I doubt it, but I've got a bad feeling. Get ready. My instincts are rarely wrong, unfortunately," said Shirai with a shrug.

The Puppets' attack was still ongoing, proving more and more of a threat.

Normally, the Puppets wouldn't be a match for a Phantom Rank's Bride. There was a glaringly obvious difference in power, so long as the Brides weren't holding back, like White Princess had been in the ruins. The Grooms were a different story, though.

For example, take a rain of a thousand needles aimed only at the Groom. What would happen if they kept switching out attackers, pummeling them constantly?

The defender would tire.

That was the Puppets' strategy.

They must hate this, Kou thought as he continued fending off attacks.

Before, they'd laughed and said Pandemonium was the only opponent worth their time. He was sure they wouldn't choose this method if they could help it. But at the same time, this was their true nature.

It was an extreme contradiction.

They continued to hold the Phantom Ranks at bay, reluctantly making use of their natural fighting style.

The other Phantom Ranks' attention was mostly focused on the Puppets' countless attacks. But Kou was different. While White Princess guarded him, he focused entirely on the *something*.

"What do you think, Kou? Have you figured anything out?" she asked.

"...No, not yet. I'm not seeing anything."

This was one of the cards in his opponent's hand. He needed as much information as he could get.

And that's why Kou was the first to notice the change.

"Is it...singing?"

At some point, the owl wings had started flickering with blue light and emitting a soft wave of sound. It was so quiet it was difficult to make out over the sounds of fighting, but it traveled.

It was almost like singing.

As soon as Kou realized what was happening, he immediately shouted a warning.

"Sasanoe, that thing, it's already started up!"

"What?"

But it was too late.

The situation had changed dramatically.

The attack came at them from the sky.

The *something* itself hadn't moved.

Instead, Special Type kihei flew over the now-inactive magic wall.

Kihei weren't usually able to get into the Academy, but things were different now.

It was almost like the voice was controlling them.

* * *

The kihei didn't look for a landing site. They crashed down right in the middle of the students. Screams ripped through the air, crimson shot skyward. Organs splashed audibly to the ground.

The Puppets stopped. Even they hadn't seen this coming.

Helze stopped attacking and shouted, voice sharp, "Moriya, Iseult, please! Think of the Academy! Don't think you can avoid blame for this!"

"Silence! In the end, they should have all died in the previous Gloaming! Besides, you Puppets are the ones who kept the regular students from fleeing!"

Helze gasped as Kou committed the names to memory.

Moriya...and Iseult...

All the while, the massacre continued.

The kihei that had appeared were indiscriminately attacking students. Kou bit his lip.

If they had a hand in the Gloaming, then it's only natural they can control both humans and kihei, too! I should have known! To think they were able to call it all the way from the ruins... The range for controlling humans seems to be limited to the Academy grounds, but the range for kihei seems far larger...

"Crimson Princess!"

"As you wish."

As Kou was lost in regret, Sasanoe made his move. On his orders, Crimson Princess tried to unleash a drill attack, but there were too many students in the way. Most of them would be turned to mincemeat if she let loose with an area attack.

"Tsk, we'll just have to get up close!"

Sasanoe rushed forward, sword in hand. Kou took one of White Princess's feathers and followed.

Just then, Shirai shouted at them.

"Stop! You're going in too straight!"

Kou didn't understand what he meant, but it became clear a moment later.

Their enemy could control both kihei and humans. That hadn't changed. It was only a few seconds, but that was plenty of time for the regular students to aim their blades at Sasanoe's sides as he rushed in to kill the Special Type.

They were just knives, but they pierced his body all the same.

He came to a stop, coughing up blood. Blade after blade was pulled from his body.

Kou was right behind him, taken aback. *How am I standing here unharmed?*

Suddenly, he heard a rasping voice.

"Kou…? It's really you, Kou…"

Kou came to a realization. It seemed that, this time, the enemy had even less control over the people it was manipulating. Several students were running away of their own free will. And in the middle of all this was a figure with their arms spread wide.

It was then that Kou noticed.

The figure was that of a girl, and she was protecting him.

Hesitantly, he turned his violet eyes in her direction.

And there stood Asagiri, guarding Kou from the knives.

One was jammed into her stomach.

"Asa…giri…?"

"A moment ago, I heard the name Kou Kaguro… I came over and… I'm glad…"

The knife was pulled out, the shock sending the mask toppling from her face.

She collapsed where she stood. Her chestnut-colored eyes filled with tears as she looked up at him. A sweet, innocent smile appeared on her lips. "Kou…," she whispered gently. "You're alive… And you didn't die, this time…"

"Asagiri… Asagiri!"

He took her hand. At the same time, someone else crouched down beside her.

Kou looked up to see Isumi, who tore off his mask. His usual annoyed expression was gone, replaced with wide-eyed shock.

He shouted, desperate, "Hey, Asagiri! I followed you here, and this is what I find?! Hey, Kou, why are you here, alive...? You're alive, but now... Asagiri is dead... What the hell is going on, Kou?!"

Isumi was berating him with panicked questions, but Kou could only shake his head in shock. He took an unsteady step forward, looking around with glazed eyes.

He couldn't really hear anything.

He only vaguely acknowledged his surroundings.

White Princess was on guard, her wings spread.

Shirai had clenched his fists.

Yurie was speaking with Sister in a sweet voice.

Crimson Princess's wings were still spread. She was completely frozen in place.

Sasanoe pressed down on a particularly deep wound and whispered.

"This, too, is how you repay us?"

He glared painfully up into the sky.

Crimson Princess ran over to him, the Bride lifting her Groom in her arms. His body went limp.

She opened her mouth, then closed it. She didn't say anything. Her arms squeezed ever more tightly around him, like she was protecting a sleeping child—a maternal gesture.

But then she changed.

Her silver wings swirled into a vortex.

Kou realized what was happening.

She was going to attack the *something*, and she didn't care who else got hurt in the process.

Before he could think, Kou was shouting. "No, Crimson Princess! This wouldn't make Sasanoe happy!"

A moment later, her attack stopped.

Blood poured from her abdomen.

Nameless had stabbed her.

* * *

"What...?"

Kou murmured, dazed.

Organic components fell to the ground before his eyes.

Along with it, a fluid that looked like blood.

Just like organs.

Or maybe like flower petals.

The sudden, horrible sight robbed Kou of speech, leaving him to stare mutely.

For a moment, he wondered if the enemy had even managed to gain control of Nameless, but that didn't seem to be the case. Crimson Princess's body fell, and Shirai caught it in his arms.

"...Sorry. Sasanoe wouldn't have wanted the students massacred. But you...who Sasanoe loved more than anyone... This was the only way to stop you, wasn't it?"

His voice was so soft.

He lifted Crimson Princess's body and carried it over to Sasanoe's, still where it had fallen when Crimson Princess dropped it. Shirai laid her down and closed his eyes as if in prayer, right in the middle of the battlefield.

"I will follow you later," he whispered. "You may hate me for this, but please wait for me."

His words were kind.

His decision to take her life had come only after considering and rejecting every other option.

Unable to do anything, Kou felt a burning in his chest.

Why did Shirai have to be forced to make that decision? Why did Crimson Princess have to die? Why did Sasanoe have to die?

Kou's jaw clenched so hard a molar cracked. His heart raced, and he felt sick.

Why did Asagiri have to protect me? Why did Tsubaki, and Yaguruma, and everyone...our Pandemonium, who tried to protect everyone, who survived the Gloaming?!

His mind filled with white-hot rage, which grew into a seething headache. He bit down harder on his lip, splitting it.

That *something* above him was still flashing.

Kou suddenly stood and roared, "White Princess!"

"Yes, Kou, I know."

She came to him and wrapped her arms around him, then spread her mechanical wings. Without a moment's hesitation, she flew straight toward that *something*. The wind rushing past struck Kou's cheeks, scattering his tears into the air. He raised his sword. The *something* was floating in the air in front of him, hidden beneath its cloth.

They closed in on it.

It didn't flee.

Kou swung his sword.

The torn cloth fell away.

Kou stared at the figure, now revealed.

"You..."

Those misty eyes stared at Kou.

Her lips curled oddly. Her mouth opened, and shrill laughter poured out.

The sound reverberated, dreadfully sinister, just like the bell that marked the arrival of the Gloaming.

The next moment, an owl feather pierced Kou's chest.

He squeezed his eyes shut.

Then opened them.

* * *

"The makeup team is running out of pigment stock. What will we do?"

"... If I recall, the Department of Exploration has some leaves that can be used to make more. I'll go get some."

"Oh, that's wonderful. Thank you, Yaguruma."

"Does anyone know where my box of nails is? I've been running around helping everyone, and I don't know where it went."

"Once you're done, Hikami, you should come help the costume team. We are always shorthanded. And Kou looks like he's spacing out... Actually, he doesn't look too good. Are you okay, Kou?"

Tsubaki gently waved a hand in front of his face.

Kou blinked.

Cloth and thread danced around them. Even nails and wood flew through the air.

"Oh, enough already!" said Kagura. "I don't even want to lecture anymore; I want to help out. I'm pretty good at making props! Am I not allowed to help? Is it against the rules?" No one was listening to his lecture. Everyone's attention was focused on preparing for the festival.

Kou listened to the ruckus. He'd missed that sound.

Everyone, all of them. They were all alive.

He looked around. Sasanoe wasn't there. He must still be skipping class, but he was probably alive, as well. The battle with Central Headquarters hadn't happened yet.

Kou felt tears well up in his eyes.

"...I made it back."

"Back where?" asked Tsubaki.

Kou stared at her intently, mind flashing back to what he'd been told. *"Tsubaki and Yaguruma are dead."*

He reached out his arms and drew Tsubaki into a tight hug. Silence fell around them. After a few seconds, Tsubaki tried to bounce out of his arms, but he wouldn't let go.

Flustered, she said, "Wh-what are you doing, Kou? I'm not sure where this came from or what it means..."

"......"

Kou wasn't able to form a reply.

Once, during his fifteen thousand repetitions, he had even killed her. But now that they'd survived the Gloaming, her death had been much harder for him to face.

The Princesses both closed their mouths when they saw how Kou was acting. They were going to try to say something, as his Brides, but they chose silence instead. They hugged him from behind, and even Tsubaki reached her small arms around him.

She squeezed him back and said, "Come on, what's wrong? You're being a moron. If there's something on your mind, you can tell me. I'll listen."

"...I had a nightmare. You were stabbed and died."

"Oh. That must have been a painful dream," she replied softly. She didn't laugh at him or say it was just a dream. She simply accepted his fear.

Mirei gently stroked his head. Hikami reached out a hand and tousled his hair. Yaguruma hesitated, then he, too, joined in.

In an instant, Kou had wrapped his arms tightly around him.

Yaguruma's eyes grew wide in surprise. "What? Did...I die, too? I don't like that."

"Don't die anymore, Yaguruma."

"Of course not, Kou," replied Yaguruma with a smile. "After seeing how upset it's making you, I can't go down so easily." But in reality, that's just how it had happened.

He'd been killed by a regular student.

Kou bit his lip and held his tongue as he released Yaguruma.

He gave everyone a smile.

The Princesses were standing next to him. "Kou, did you come back in time?" whispered White Princess.

"What in the world happened...?" Black Princess asked next.

"I did. It was like...a nightmare turned real."

His Brides hugged him again. He hugged them back, then stood up and dashed off while everyone watched him.

He pulled open the classroom door. Kagura didn't stop him, probably guessing something was up.

He left the classroom behind and rushed through the Academy, heading toward the teachers' lounge. Just like Pandemonium's dorms, it was a converted guest room in Central Headquarters. The teacher not in charge of the current lecture waited there.

Kou pulled open the lavish door.

He stood facing the person inside, then said, "'Turn and peel away the skin.' That's the message you asked me to deliver. You also said, 'What we need in this situation isn't me as a teacher.' And finally, I have a request."

Kou stared directly at Hibiya.

Then he continued, "You stopped me from exploring Central Headquarters before, but the situation has changed. Please help me. For Pandemonium's sake, I will cease to be who I was. I know how to use my ability to its fullest now, and I've got the information we need for a different outcome. So—"

"That's enough. Quiet."
Hibiya shook their head and took a cigarette from their chest pocket.
Kou bit his lip, afraid it hadn't worked.
But in a smooth voice, Hibiya replied:

"Tell me everything... What hell did you see?"

Kou Kaguro gave a single nod.
Then he began to describe the worst possible outcome.

The Bride of Demise

12. AN ALLY OF JUSTICE

Kou Kaguro thought about his situation.

He thought about what he'd lost.

He'd traveled back in time, back from the worst possible outcome. He was the only person who had seen what had happened there. There was no one who could truly share that sadness, that pain, those tragic memories.

Memories of Tsubaki, Yaguruma, Sasanoe, and Crimson Princess dying, memories of everything breaking.

It weighed him down with a heavy despair.

It had been the same with his fifteen thousand repetitions. Most of that time was his burden to bear—and his alone.

Facing this fact head-on was enough to gnaw away at Kou's spirit. To be honest, it was strange he hadn't broken during his fifteen thousand repetitions. The only reason he was able to get through it was because he wasn't human, and the emotional numbness that came with that became a strength.

Kou lay on the bed in his room, his eyes closed.

Now, however, he felt his heart would shatter if he didn't talk about what he had experienced.

And so he talked of his sorrow.

The Princesses nodded as they listened to his nightmare.

"That's horrible... A future where everyone dies is too awful to bear."

"You've been through so much, Kou... You've seen hell itself. I'm glad you made it back from that."

They gently stroked his head.

Kou clung to the warmth of his Brides' fingers. But at the same time, he realized a terrible truth.

If I keep using this ability, eventually I'll break.

People weren't meant to repeat time fifteen thousand times. He had made it through for White Princess's sake, but he'd already exceeded his limit. Continuing now was dangerous.

"...But now I have the chance to change fate," muttered Kou through clenched teeth. His gaze harbored a resolve as hard as steel.

He sat up, and looked both Princesses in the eyes.

He'd already spoken to Hibiya and Kagura.

"White Princess, Black Princess," he began, his tone serious. "I want to ask you both a favor."

His Brides nodded without a hint of hesitation.

* * *

After finishing his talk with the Princesses, Kou left the room. He wanted a drink of water, and he wanted to be alone.

He walked unsteadily to the cafeteria.

It'd been a long time since he'd gone out alone like this. He'd stopped exploring after Hibiya warned him, and there was always someone with him during festival preparations. That had been fun. But right now, the quiet, empty hallway was gentle on his frayed nerves.

Once he got to the cafeteria, he glanced around at the empty seats. He picked up a pitcher of water from a table, poured himself a glass, and chugged the water down. He shook his head and sighed.

He washed the glass before turning around.

Just then, something strange happened.

A girl in strange dress stood before him. She had a sheet draped over her head.

It was the lost girl he'd run into during the festival.

Kou's eyes narrowed as he wondered what was going on. Why was she here?

And what's more, she reminded him of the strange thing he had encountered in the worst possible outcome. They had a similar shape, though this girl didn't have owl wings poking out from under her sheet. He couldn't see her face or hair.

Voice oddly stiff, the girl addressed Kou. "Um… I just wanted to be an ally of justice."

"What was that…?"

Her words were sudden, but there was something in her voice that sounded earnest. He couldn't tease her or laugh at her. She had said it with the same gravity as a love confession.

Next, she posed a question. "What about you…? Do you think I'm weird?"

"…I don't think you're weird. I agree; I feel the same way."

Kou clenched his fists and answered the girl's question with heartfelt sincerity.

"I want to be an ally of justice, too. I'll become one for the sake of my friends."

The girl appeared to be smiling. She reached out a small hand and stroked Kou's cheek with a white palm. He still couldn't see her face. But her voice was full of joy as she said, "Oh, really…? I thought so. I don't have the freedom to choose. They won't let me choose not to do it. But ever since you survived the Gloaming, I thought you might be that kind of person. That's why I wanted to meet you, just once."

"Freedom to choose? the Gloaming?"

Kou narrowed his eyes.

And then the girl whispered.

"………………………………………………………I'm so jealous."

There was clear hatred in her voice. Hatred directed at someone. Kou glanced over his shoulder to see if anyone was there, but he didn't see anyone.

When he turned back, the girl was gone. There was nowhere she could hide in the cafeteria. It was almost like she'd never existed. Either that or she had disappeared into another space.

Kou cocked his head, confused.

In the end, however, he decided not to dwell on the girl's existence. He had a feeling that if he did, he wouldn't be able to move forward.

The Bride of Demise

13. I AM ALONE

It was ten days before the festival. Night had fallen on Central Headquarters.

Kou Kaguro, White Princess, Black Princess, and Shuu Hibiya headed out together to explore.

The four moved through the night's gloom without a sound.

Quietly, Kou spoke to his Brides. "All right, you two. You can use your kihei abilities. Don't let them find you."

"Understood, Kou. I won't hold you back."

"…It is okay. We can move much faster than humans. No one will discover us."

Kou referred to the map in his memory as the four moved farther into the building.

The deeper they went into the building, the sparser the decorations became, gradually exposing the building's functionality.

They weren't heading toward any specific location, but there was a specific point and a specific being they were aiming for. When they arrived at the spot where Hibiya had stopped Kou before, Kou's feet ceased moving.

He turned back to ask permission from his second teacher. "Is it all right?"

"Yes, go."

Hibiya nodded, and Kou hurried on.

Ahead was an area that Kou visited since Hibiya returned to the Academy. The building's walls slowly gave way to relics left from the prehistoric period. The four never stopped moving as they traversed the strange space. For now, nothing stood in their way. Not long after, however, they ran across what they had been looking for.

"Even you, Hibiya, felt like taking a stroll around Central Headquarters? That's a bit dangerous, don't you think?"

"The Puppets, huh?" said Hibiya calmly. "*You're late.* I want you to let us pass... And I have a few things I want to ask. That's why I took the trouble." Kou, on the other hand, held his breath.

"*If we go farther into the Central Headquarters, it will likely end in a fight with the Puppets.*"

Hibiya had predicted as much earlier. Even so, what had awaited them was far beyond his expectations.

The Puppets were in impossible locations. On the floor, the walls, the ceiling. Their shadows were cast in all directions.

Faced with their outpouring of hostility, Kou came to a realization.

It looks like Hibiya's warning was spot-on.

Running into the Puppets at night in Central Headquarters would put him at a distinct disadvantage. And if he'd failed to heed that warning and run into them, there was a high probability he would have been subjected to a brief conversation and then instantly killed.

The Puppets could defeat kihei without magic armor. During Kou's second battle with them, they had used regular students as shields. But now Kou was realizing that even that wasn't their true nature.

Now he had no choice but to see it.

The Puppets' real skill was assassination.

They were likely best at indoor battles. No matter what direction they came from, Kou would die instantly. The experience he'd gained through his fifteen thousand repetitions allowed him to sense that naturally.

Hibiya wasn't shaken, however, not even in the face of multiple opponents.

They spoke with the Puppets as casually as if they'd run into them on a stroll.

"I've heard there are some of you more hostile toward Pandemonium than is necessary. I want you to tell me the specifics. I just want some verification while we're fighting... You're still on the principal's side, aren't you? It shouldn't cost you anything."

"And it won't gain us anything, either. We have been asked to subsume Kou Kaguro and White Princess into the Puppets to the extent possible. Could you make that happen?"

"What are you talking about? Of course you'll gain something. You'll be able to walk away from this without me beating you into a bloody pulp."

"Of course... You haven't changed one bit," said Helze, voice heavy and full of mixed emotions. Then she said something Kou didn't expect. "You're just the same as when you were our teacher."

"That's right," Hibiya responded in a singsong voice. "Just like now, I tend to use my power to get what I want, so they moved me to Pandemonium. I was a bit too hard to control to stay in charge of you all."

The next moment, one of the shadows moved, and Harusaki was standing behind Hibiya.

Her words came with a fist as fast as sound.

"I'm sorry, my teacher."

"You're the only one I gave personal lessons...but you still leave so many openings."

Hibiya grabbed Harusaki's fist. Then, using her arm as a pivot, tossed her to the ground. The next moment, Hibiya snapped her arm without a moment's hesitation, rendering her powerless.

Battle erupted.

Attacks came from every direction. Hibiya lashed out with a whiplike kick, deflecting a shower of flying daggers. They then crouched down to evade the slash of a katana before, unbelievably, blocking a bullet with the back of their hand. Without stopping, they grabbed the arm of a nearby student and broke it in one fluid motion.

"Gah, agh!"

"Sorry, I need you for a second."

Hibiya took the now powerless student and used them as a shield against the other Puppets' attacks.

Several students were forced to move in for close combat and ended up on the floor one after another.

Kou stood staring at the scene in disbelief.

It was like a child playing. Everything felt like a joke. But it was actually a display of incredible skill and speed.

Hibiya was fast and highly skilled. They didn't even need their Bride.

That's when Kou had a realization.

This is what "Turn and peel away the skin" was referring to.

Shuu Hibiya's true form wasn't that of a teacher.

They, too, were an assassin.

At last, the battle was decided.

The Puppets lay on the ground.

Hibiya stood before Helze. "All right, tell me," they said coldly. "It wouldn't do to kill you all, and I don't want to, either."

"Oh, fine… I imagine you've already guessed, though. It's Moriya and Iseult's faction."

"I knew it. If that's the case, I can leave the rest to Kagura."

Hibiya crossed their arms, and Kou nodded. They'd already spoken to Kagura on their way here, and they'd be leaving the higher-ups, Moriya and Iseult, to him.

Meanwhile, Kou and Hibiya were to handle the *something*.

Helze gave a low chuckle. "…You really are the same," she said to Hibiya. "You never change. Even now, you look like you want to alter fate… You don't even think of us as your students anymore, do you?"

"I am an assassin," said Hibiya. "My true nature hasn't changed, not back then, not now. Don't expect anything from me. Dwelling on the past won't help any of you… How many times have we said our farewells now?"

"Good-bye, Puppets," they continued. "Report our actions to your heart's content. But I do pray you'll choose a path that is good for the Academy."

There was no response.

Hibiya began to walk away, leaving students groaning in pain in their wake.

They came up to Kou and stopped to say something.

The same thing that Kagura had said when they spoke earlier.

"All right, Kou Kaguro. You'll have to handle what lies ahead."

* * *

"If that's the case, there are still things we can do. All right, Kou Kaguro. You'll have to handle what lies ahead."

This was after Kou had traveled back, right after he'd asked Hibiya for help.

Once again, he and Kagura were in the empty classroom.

Kagura's back straightened when he heard the names Moriya and Iseult. He could do something about two higher-ups like them running wild. The next moment, though, Kagura scrunched down again, his shoulders slouching as he peered into Kou's eyes.

Their gazes met. "No matter how advanced the magic technology being used," said Kagura, "it would be difficult for modern humans to control people... They'd need a fairly powerful kihei. Which means the source of their control is that *something* you saw. It's got to be in Central Headquarters somewhere... And if that's the case, you just need to use Millennium Black Princess."

It would surely respond to her.

So Kagura had said. Kou didn't fully understand what he had meant. But he did sense one thing. While Black Princess's power may be waning, she was still the queen of the kihei. And just like White Princess, she was the "nonexistent" seventh member of the Princess Series.

If this something *is a kihei, it might respond to Black Princess's call.*

Kou also had an important piece of information about this *something*. He'd seen what was underneath the cloth, after it was torn.

A kihei in the form of a little girl.

That something *was a Princess Series.*

But she probably didn't correspond to any of the confirmed numbers. So then, what was she? The details were unknown.

They only knew one thing.

In all likelihood, that *something* was the cause of the Gloaming. If so, its ability was the antithesis of Curtain Call, which had been made to end all wars.

And in that case, they still had a chance to win.

* * *

After his conversation with Kagura, Kou had explained the situation to the Princesses.

Then he had enlisted Hibiya's help and brought the two Princesses with him deep into Central Headquarters. If they wanted to reach the *something*, they would have to traverse the hidden areas.

The farther they went, the more likely it was to respond.

In the darkness, Kou called out to Black Princess. "I don't think we'll be able to get physically close to the room it's in. But are you able to sense something as we're running around?"

"...I hadn't noticed it before. But after listening to you and coming this far, I can tell. There's something here."

"What is it?"

"A kihei that isn't a Bride," murmured Black Princess. She stopped running, and her form began to change.

Her uniform morphed into a black dress, and her crow-like wings appeared. The chains binding them came undone, and she spread them wide. Now, looking like the queen of the kihei, Millennium Black Princess reached her arms forward.

She spoke in a whisper as she searched the space around them. "If I look for it, I can tell... There is someone hidden here. Oh, this is..."

"Amazing, Black Princess. I don't have that kind of search function... Hmm, or do I?"

"Ah, it's calling out," said Millennium Black Princess, nodding.

A moment later, the hallway's inorganic walls warped drastically. Kou's vision swam and changed.

Then it dawned on Kou what was happening.

The *something* had forcefully called out to them. When Black Princess noticed its presence and reached out her hands, it had tried to reach back, and it had pulled them in.

At the same time, Kou realized that no matter how much they explored Central Headquarters, they would have never gotten here.

They had been drawn into a completely different space.

Kou closed his eyes for a moment, drew in a breath, and let it out.

Kou Kaguro opened his violet eyes.

He was surrounded by a heavy, almost viscous darkness. Everything around him was filled with that swirling blackness, except for a single point. There was one spot that shone with a pale-blue light. Unfamiliar inorganic walls curved up into the darkness.

The light emanated from something strange.

A pair of organic wings that looked ready to fall apart.

The wings resembled an owl's and pulsated with blue light. They were deformed. Between the stiff-looking feathers ran countless veinlike cables.

The wings were spread wide on each side. They weren't mounted on the wall, but they were perfectly still, not moving in the slightest.

Kou slowly turned his gaze.

His eyes slid down the smooth curve of the wings to where they attached.

In between them stood a girl, the wings growing out of her back.

Her white skin was like a corpse's, her purple hair like a finely crafted wig.

"…Who are you?" asked Kou.

The girl didn't reply.

Without a word, she opened her eyes.

Those misty eyes stared at Kou. He was relieved; she seemed able to understand him. But the next moment, her lips curled oddly. Her mouth opened, and shrill laughter poured out.

The sound reverberated, dreadfully sinister, just like the bell that marked the arrival of the Gloaming.

* * *

"I… We know this person," said White Princess. "Her information is stored within us because she is our enemy."

"She was assumed lost and broken," said Black Princess. "She is the lost number five."

The two Princesses together revealed the strange form's identity.

Number five of the Princess Series, who had been lost. Kou remembered hearing about her. His eyes opened wide.

Beside him, Black Princess pressed her hands to her head. It seemed she was suffering from a severe headache.

Eventually, she shook her head and groaned, "I lost certain information during the course of my repetitions. White Princess? Do you remember?"

"Now that I'm looking at her, the stimulus has activated my memory retrieval... Her alias is Opening Ceremony. She has the power to upset the magic inside a human or especially a kihei, robbing them of their volition and bending them to her will. She is our enemy, who was supposedly destroyed."

What was this lost number five? The two Princesses put it into words:

"She is a being who can start wars."

Kou guessed that these details weren't given to any of the other Princesses, including Crimson Princess. This information had been provided to Curtain Call alone, as she was made to end all wars, and this being was thus her enemy.

Opening Ceremony was made and likely also destroyed in the prehistoric period.

He felt certain there had been a complicated political situation in the background of those events.

Afterward, she had slept.

But she was rediscovered.

Even among the higher-ups, only some of them knew about her. That was apparent, as there were even some who had surmised Millennium Black Princess was actually the lost number five. Opening Ceremony had been kept secret on the surface, while being used as a means to instigate the Gloaming.

At the same time, she was ordered by Moriya and Iseult to secretly manipulate regular students into reducing Pandemonium's power. Kou's thoughts raced as he came to grips with this.

I can understand killing off some of Pandemonium, to an extent... But why cause the Gloaming? What could possibly make it necessary to manufacture such a horrific tragedy?

Thinking about it brought him no answer. There was only one thing he was certain of.

His only option was to destroy Opening Ceremony, the lost number five.

He had to destroy her until there was nothing left.

The Princess Series had personalities, and it was likely that she wasn't causing these tragedies, including the Gloaming, because she wanted to. Behind everything was the will of living humans. That was certain. It was not the lost number five they should hate.

But he couldn't let her live.

Kou Kaguro had struggled through the Gloaming fifteen thousand times, and he could never allow that hell to exist. As long as she was being used as a mechanism to bring it about, he had no other choice.

Kou took one of White Princess's feathers. Either of the Princesses would do the deed if he gave the order, but Kou didn't want to ask them to kill one of their own. That would be too cruel.

Without a word, Kou raised the feather.

The lost number five didn't move.

After her loud laughter subsided, she had fallen silent.

Her misty eyes stared at Kou.

But the moment before his blade fell, she opened her mouth.

"……………………………………………………………………………Unfair."

"Huh?"

The next moment, her owl wings gave a powerful flap. The wind sent Kou flying backward.

White Princess quickly snatched him from the side as he flew back, then Black Princess held on to both of them. In front of them, the lost number five began to glow with blue light. Red tears streamed from her large eyes. "I'm alone. I'm always alone, all all all all aLl alLallaLL ALL, all alone!" she shrieked. Her voice was filled with sorrow and fury.

She folded her wings and leaped. For a moment, she spiraled in the air, before disappearing from Kou's and the Princesses' sight. She'd flown high above them.

In no time, there was an explosive sound from above. The ceiling had been shattered.

Rubble fell to the ground.

Kou ran over to the hole in the ceiling. Looking up, he could see a circle of night sky peeking through far in the distance.

The lost number five had fled.

But that, too, had been accounted for in their plans.

The Bride of Demise

14. KOU KAGURO'S DECISION

Silence had fallen over the school at night, but several shadows flitted through the darkness.

Kou and the Princesses flew up through the courtyard and into the sky. They had used White Princess's mechanical wings to exit through the hole in the ceiling created by the lost number five. It looked like the underground space they had just occupied had been directly below the courtyard.

White Princess twirled and slowed, lowering all three of them onto the lawn.

Kou looked up. The lost number five was floating in the night sky, silhouetted against the moon. In a way, she looked like an injured owl.

He turned his eyes back toward the ground. He could see people lined up in front of Central Headquarters. These were the members of Pandemonium—Kou had asked them to come earlier.

Mirei, Hikami, Tsubaki, and Yaguruma stood ahead of the others. Kou ran toward their familiar faces.

"Everyone ready?" he asked, tone serious. "It's just like I told you before. Don't lose focus. There's a chance she can overrule your consciousness if you give her an opening. Keep that in mind."

"I still don't really understand…but I'm assuming that's the enemy?" asked Mirei as she pointed above them. Kou nodded.

At the same time, he thought back over his assumption.

As long as you don't lose focus, as people had at the festival, it shouldn't be able to take control.

When Pandemonium's Phantom Ranks had abandoned the Academy, the lost number five wasn't able to make them attack each other. Humans didn't have much magic. Unlike kihei, unless a human gave up a certain amount of their consciousness, it would be difficult to upset their internal magic enough to take over control.

That's why she'd tended to aim for the closing of the festival, when the students were the most unguarded.

The lost number five gently flapped her wings.

There were no regular students here. If she tried to control anyone in the dorms, it would take time for them to come out. This was their only opportunity to put an end to this.

Sasanoe stepped forward. Yurie followed him gracefully, and Shirai had an imposing air as he stepped forward, too.

"I don't know the details," murmured Sasanoe, "but according to Kagura, that's Pandemonium's enemy."

His words signaled Crimson Princess, and she spread her liquid silver wings.

Without warning, she launched an attack over their heads. Hundreds of silver bullets twinkled in the moonlight as they flew toward lost number five. The hit was so direct that it almost looked as if the target was sucking in the bullets.

A rain of blood showered down.

A scream tore through the sky.

A moment later, lost number five spread her owl wings wide.

Kou could hear a cry.

That voice…

It reached far into the distance.

Far, far, to the edges of the earth.

It sounded like singing.

"White Princess!"

"I know, Kou. Take my hand."

He took her hand, and she slipped her other arm around his waist. Once again, they soared into the air. Kou glanced through the darkness, to the other side of the magic wall.

While he had suspected this would happen, he still gasped when he saw the horrifying result.

In the distance, the horizon turned black, as if another night was bubbling up from the earth.

Strange forms like insects, like beasts, like machines, stained the world.

The kihei horde had appeared.

This time, they wouldn't be able to prepare. The magic wall did not wake.

Swarms of kihei grabbed onto the Academy's outer wall. The alarm rang. Screams of shock and fear erupted from around the Academy.

Kou could tell from the sound. The students' reactions were within the normal range. There didn't seem to be any students under lost number five's control. She was putting everything she had into controlling the kihei.

In response to her call, masses of kihei began scaling the wall.

Kou couldn't help but mutter, "It's just like the Gloaming…"

That nightmare had risen up again.

But just then, Kou saw a shadowy figure atop the wall. It was a man wearing a worn coat over his military uniform—Kagura.

Kagura lifted his arm in the air, and something fluttered there. They were black feathers. They swirled into a spiral, and he whispered, "…Burst."

He snapped his fingers once, and hundreds of kihei exploded.

Kou nodded. It was as incredible as ever.

Kagura lowered his arm, then moved one finger.

"Kou Kaguro, can you hear me?" came a voice. Kou looked to see a single black feather floating in front of his nose. The voice was coming from the feather. Kagura continued, tone carefree, "I've drawn away half of the kihei that made it to the Academy. This Gloaming doesn't work like the real thing. It's not a side effect of the queen's magic going berserk. Instead, each individual kihei's magic is being sent out of control. That means it can't go on forever. The lost number five should have her limits. And we should be able to stop the rampage by destroying her."

He was telling Kou and the others what to do—leaving it in their hands.

Kou nodded. Kagura raised his arm again. Black feathers rushed through the night sky. As the darkness danced to Kagura's whims, he whispered, "Good luck."

The same words he'd said back then.

Kou nodded again and descended to the ground. To Pandemonium, he said, "As you can tell from the alarm, hordes of kihei are on their way here. I'd like all of you to intercept them."

"Of course. We are Pandemonium."

Mirei, Hikami, Tsubaki, and Yaguruma nodded. The others rolled up their sleeves.

The members of Pandemonium already knew.

A new battle was beginning on the Academy grounds.

* * *

"This is an emergency announcement. I repeat: All regular students must remain indoors. I repeat: All regular students must remain indoors. This order applies to the Department of Combat as well. I repeat: All regular students..."

Shuu Hibiya's voice tore through the night air. They were broadcasting throughout the Academy, probably without permission.

Kou nodded.

This would allow Pandemonium to fight without their Brides being seen. There were other problems, however. There were a lot of kihei coming over the walls. It would be hard to take care of them all if they spread throughout the Academy. Thankfully, that concern turned out to be unwarranted.

All the kihei were heading in the same direction—straight for White Princess and Black Princess.

"I see...," murmured White Princess. "Do you really feel it's that unfair?"

The lost number five clearly felt the Princesses were her enemies.

First came a Special Type. In response, a Full Humanoid Bride was freed from his chains and rushed toward it. This was Mirei's Bride, My Kitty. He closed in on the strange form, its entire body rippling.

Mirei's voice was calm. "...Set."

This time, My Kitty was using his own chains as a weapon. He wrapped them around what appeared to be the other kihei's neck and immediately began pulling with precise strength.

"...End it."

There was a dull crack, and the Special Type's neck snapped.

But the next instant, something spewed acid at My Kitty. It was an attack from a different Special Type, aiming for the opening in My Kitty's defenses as he landed. A tall wall sprouted up, guarding My Kitty from the acid—the work of Tsubaki's Bride, Doll's Guardian.

She stood on his shoulder, building up protective walls. In a singsong voice, she warned, "Don't let your guard down, Mirei. This is a battlefield now. Those who lose focus die first."

"You're right. Thank you, Tsubaki. I'll have to give this my all." Mirei patted her cheeks. She looked at My Kitty, and her eyes filled with love. "My darling beloved, I am so glad you weren't harmed."

Next to her stood Hikami, pressing a hand to his forehead. Beside him was one small piece of Unknown. "Ah, thank you, my beloved wife...," he murmured after some time. "I've got a report. There's a Type A on the east side. To the west is a group of Special Types. We also need to spread our groups around and set up a strong defensive line on the west side... The courtyard terrain is too complicated. First things first, we need to relocate to the square."

"Yes, let's do that...," agreed Yaguruma. "There's a risk of my Bride's flames getting out of control here." Kou and the Princesses nodded. Hikami went to report the same information to their other classmates.

Pandemonium moved out. They cut down a Type A in their path and gathered in the square.

But once there, they saw something unexpected.

The three Phantom Ranks were already at work.

"Now, Sister! There are so many bad little boys and girls. Oh, so many. Punish them. And then return to your peaceful rest with me."

Yurie's Sister launched her steel wires. With each attack, ten or more kihei were strung up in the air.

Yurie was still in her pajamas, a stuffed animal in her arms. Despite being in the middle of a fierce battle, she never lost her dreamy smile. Every once in a while, Sister would glance at her lovingly.

"How annoying," said Shirai with a heavy sigh. "Not getting a good night's sleep will have a negative impact on my training... This is far from ideal." His Bride, Nameless, smashed its formless body into a group of kihei, engulfing over ten of them. Shirai nodded as he watched his Bride at work.

Crimson Princess fired a spray of silver bullets, turning a large number of kihei into Swiss cheese. Sasanoe rushed through the gaps between them, cutting down kihei one after another.

White Princess joined the Phantom Ranks.

"I will go, too. Curtain Call has arrived."

Her mechanical wings shone. Beams of blue light burned through the ground in every direction. Right now, the Phantom Ranks' Brides weren't held back by the presence of regular students.

They were free to trample down the kihei with their overwhelming power.

Kou watched them. *This is the real Pandemonium*, he thought.

He held back his tears. *But...* He turned to look toward the sky. There was a flash of blue light. An attack rained down, very similar to White Princess's, boring into the earth.

* * *

"...Ugh, is everyone okay?" called Hikami.

"Making a barrier overhead is quite difficult, but I'd expect nothing less of my Doll's Guardian," said Tsubaki quietly.

Everyone who could make barriers reacted quickly, covering the group from overhead. A few people cut through the blue light on their own, deflecting it as it fell. However, a second attack would be pushing their limits.

Hikami clucked his tongue in annoyance. "That attack sure is a handful. Did it come from the thing above us?"

"Um, Hikami, could you...?"

"What is it, Mirei?"

"Um, why are you covering me?"

"Huh?"

Hikami was covering Mirei from above, protecting her from the overhead attack.

Kou knew. He'd been the only one to witness it, but Hikami had covered Mirei when Millennium Black Princess had killed them all. He'd also tried to protect her during the worst possible outcome of the festival.

Hikami blinked several times. After thinking it over, and then over again, he eventually said, "It just, sort of, happened."

"Ever since that girl asked you out...," said Mirei, seeming uncomfortable. "Sorry, we were following you. But I've been wondering ever since… What am I to you?"

This wasn't the place for that sort of conversation, but Tsubaki, Yaguruma, Kou, and the two Princesses were all frozen for a few moments. They all felt as if some incredibly important exchange were taking place in front of them.

Hikami flapped his arms about meaninglessly, opened and closed his mouth, then clenched his fists and said, "My…very good…friend?"

"Friend?"

"F-friend. Is that bad?"

"No, that's good. Let's keep it like that."

Tsubaki tsked; Yaguruma shouted in disappointment. Kou nodded in deep agreement. But it looked like Hikami and Mirei's relationship was fixed in its current state.

They each turned their focus back to the battle.

Kou looked sharply above them.

The lost number five had her owl wings spread wide, and she was still singing. She released a steady rain of blue light toward the ground.

Sasanoe slashed the rain of light with his blade of liquid silver. "We've got to kill that thing while fighting the kihei?" he muttered. "This won't be easy."

"You're right. As things are, we don't have enough people," Kou agreed. The kihei had been arriving in a steady stream.

"Run, my Bride, the only one in this world to receive my kisses. My perfect Fire Horse!"

Yaguruma's Fire Horse trampled a section of the horde. The flaming horse rushed back and forth through the enemy, the flames leaping from kihei to kihei. Mirei's My Kitty continued to crack the kihei's skulls, and Tsubaki's Doll's Guardian kept forming walls, crushing enemies between them.

Every member of Pandemonium gave it their all. But they couldn't keep up with the sheer numbers of kihei.

Only Yurie, Shirai, and Sasanoe could handle the enemies coming in from all directions. If the Phantom Ranks didn't keep fighting, the Wasp and Flower Ranks would start to see casualties.

The three Phantom Ranks had to focus on continually bringing down Special Type kihei.

Kou met White Princess's eyes. He gave a short nod, then looked back at Sasanoe and said, "I'm heading out. Keep it up, Sasanoe."

"Just you two? That's foolish, but all right. Show us another win."

There was trust in Sasanoe's words.

Kou nodded, then took off across the square. But his path was blocked by a crab-shaped kihei. With a fluid strike, he slashed at the Type A kihei, splitting it in half.

On he ran, leaving its corpse in his wake. He called to his Bride.

"White Princess!"

"Yes, let's go, Kou!"

She took his hand, and the two rose up into the night sky.

* * *

They shot upward, splitting the air. Kou grit his teeth against the pressure.

White Princess shot off blue light as they flew, and lost number five fired back.

Kou cut down most of the beams.

Number five sped up. She spun through the air, firing multiple beams of blue at them. The light arched toward them, but White Princess evaded them as she flew. The lost number five's attacks were now focused entirely on the two of them. As they flew, Kou looked back to see where the shot had landed and saw that Pandemonium had managed to guard against the attack.

But Kou and White Princess weren't catching up with number five. Because White Princess was carrying Kou, number five was that much faster.

The lost number five turned to face them.

She stared at them with misty eyes. It looked like she was smiling at them—a smile filled with jealously and hate.

Kou looked into those eyes and whispered, "Okay, I need your help… Black Princess."

"I know, Kou. My wings still belong to you."

The lost number five had been so focused on Kou and White Princess that she hadn't noticed.

At some point, her enemy had positioned themselves in the direction she was flying.

Black Princess spread her wings wide.

Hovering in place, she wrapped her arms around number five, holding her.

* * *

"Ah! Agh!"

"I'm sorry, but I can't let you escape. My lovely Groom asked me not to," whispered Black Princess. She tightened her slender white arms.

The lost number five struggled wildly, as if she'd gone mad, but Black Princess wouldn't let go.

This was the perfect moment to finish her, but White Princess couldn't fire off her blue light.

If she did, Black Princess wouldn't be able to escape.

So she turned to Kou. "Do you mind, Kou?"

"I don't, White Princess."

They nodded to each other.

And Kou realized:

He wasn't afraid. He wasn't uncertain.

All he felt now was the determination to end this ceaseless nightmare.

White Princess tensed her arms, wrapped around Kou. And then she threw him forward.

With his sword in hand, he flew like a loosed arrow.

Just as he had during the worst possible outcome, he swung his sword.

The lost number five looked at him.

Tears welled up in her large eyes.

The sword made contact.

In that moment, a scene was reflected in Kou's vision.

There was a little girl walking, wearing a white hospital gown. She wasn't a kihei. She was just a human. Only her hair had been turned purple.

An adult was holding her hand, and she asked him:

"Everyone will love me when I'm the Opening Ceremony?"

The adult told her yes. He nodded, as if it was beyond question.

The girl laughed in excitement and smiled cutely.

She just wanted to help people.
She never thought her role would be to start a war.
The thought never even crossed her mind.
She had never imagined that she would be broken.
Hated by everyone.
That they would try to kill her again.

She just…

Wanted to be an ally of justice.
"Kou!"
White Princess's shout brought him back to himself.
In front of him, the lost number five was crying. Huge teardrops sparkled as they fell to the ground. She trembled, her mouth open as she frantically asked, "Why, why, why? I wanted to be loved. I loved everyone. That was all."
Kou gripped his sword tight.
And he instantly understood.
He'd met this little girl, though only twice. She'd hidden her wings and come to meet him.
The lost number five.
She'd said she wanted to be an ally of justice.
She'd spoken so earnestly of it.
But he was about to fall. If he did, this would happen all over again. He looked at the girl in front of him.

And he thought of the Gloaming.
He thought of the worst possible outcome of the festival.
He thought of his precious friends' smiling faces.

She continued to cry in front of him.
But still…
He tightly gripped his sword.

"That's all I ever—"
"…I'm sorry."

*   *   *

And Kou Kaguro made his decision.

As he passed her, he swung his blade.
Kou Kaguro cut off the head of the lost number five.

* * *

Blood spurted into the air.
Organic components fell to the ground.

The girl who wanted nothing more than to be loved was broken.

This was the result of Kou Kaguro's decision.

Kou tried to catch her organic components as they scattered, but they all spilled from his arms.

And he fell.
His tears leaped up into the air. He would crash into the ground and die.
He decided that would be fine.

After all, he'd killed that little girl.
He had made his decision and cut off her head.

Maybe Kou Kaguro deserved to be broken.

But as he fell, pale-white arms supported him. Black Princess caught him. She squeezed him close, so he wouldn't slip out.
She whispered to him, "You told me…we would live together."
"You're right, I did… I promised," he replied, clinging to her words.
Black Princess must have noticed Kou's pain. He hugged his second Bride back.
Then another voice called out to him.
"Kou, are you all right?"
White Princess flew over to his side, and his two Brides carried him, their grips firm.

The lost number five fell to the ground in his place. Her body crashed pathetically.

Kou squeezed his eyes shut. She was dead, but the people behind it all were still alive.

He bit his lip so hard it bled. Neither of the Princesses said anything.

Silence reigned for some time.

Eventually, White Princess whispered, "We did it, Kou."

"Yes… You accomplished this, Kou," added Black Princess.

"Yeah," he said.

They also knew that there were other people who deserved judgment. But for now, they had eliminated the source of at least one disaster. They tried to accept Kou's guilt into their own hearts, using their own words.

In response, Kou wiped away his overflowing tears. He struggled to squeeze his trembling voice from his throat. At last, he managed to whisper:

"It's all over."

The kihei in the square had lost their terrifying hostility.

The golden rays of the sun were rising on the other side of the wall.

The Bride of Demise

15. THE FINAL FESTIVAL

They wrapped things up quickly after that.

With their overwhelming urge to kill humans now gone, the kihei were easy to wipe out. Once they'd all been killed, Pandemonium returned to Central Headquarters and waited.

The regular students wondered who could possibly have killed that many kihei, but they had no way of finding out the answer. Time passed like nothing had happened.

Meanwhile, Kou waited with bated breath for a certain person to contact him.

And finally, in the empty classroom, Kagura called him aside.

"Using the information you provided, I was able to make it look like the lost number five went on a rampage because Moriya and Iseult's faction was trying to use her to control people for their own benefit. At her own request, there weren't any monitoring devices in the room she was kept in. That worked in our favor."

"So then, Pandemonium?"

"Won't have their lives threatened by anyone... Though, the principal's faction is a bit dangerous. Anyway, the Puppets you ran into have kept their mouths shut. I don't think we have to worry for now."

Kou felt the tension drain from his body as he listened. He finally felt alive again.

There was nothing he could do about the higher-ups' scheming. But then Kagura said something surprising.

"Well, it's not like this'll stop the Gloaming from ever happening again."

"...What do you mean?"

"Moriya and Iseult were using the lost number five to try to kill Pandemonium, but there are a lot more people causing the Gloaming," muttered Kagura.

Kou had been aware that the Gloaming was probably being caused by the combined will of many people.

And Kagura continued with even more disheartening news.

"This is just a guess based on what Black Princess said about the steps leading up to a queen's rampage, but... I think that once the lost number five had her sights set on the queen of the kihei, she would start to manipulate her in a way that would go unnoticed. First, she would cause the queen to draw magic out of the other kihei. This way, the queen would slowly accumulate magic. Then she would upset all that magic at once, allowing her to efficiently cause all kihei to rampage. Thus, the lost number five was an important trigger in bringing about the Gloaming... But we can't say for certain that they won't develop some technology to replace her in the future."

"But...if that's true, then..."

Why did he kill that little girl?

The words died in his throat. He clenched his fists. As his knuckles creaked, he asked the question that most confused him.

"Why are humans causing the Gloaming?"

It was a disaster that resulted in the deaths of most of those at the Academy.

His heart filled with rage as he spoke, but Kagura just shrugged and said, "All I can guess at this point is they're doing it to reduce the number of kihei when the population has risen too high—and to reduce Pandemonium's power when they've gotten too strong. We exist only to break the tide and protect the imperial capital. If all they have to do is intentionally break us and rebuild us a few times, it might be worth it to them."

It was just too cruel a suggestion.

And the people causing it were still alive.

Kou felt murderous rage and hatred swirl in the pit of his stomach, but they'd gotten past the immediate threat. He'd protected the people he needed to protect. He tried desperately to focus on that.

"...Could I go see Isumi and Asagiri?" he asked next.

"Uh, well, you're really not supposed to be interacting with regular students, but...it should be fine if you just talk a bit. Though..."

Kagura's tone turned cold at the end, leaving Kou confused.

The teacher looked away, putting his suspicion into words.

"Opening Ceremony's ability was consistently activated at the end of the festival. But based on what you told me, Asagiri was the only one who stabbed you at an unrelated time."

"...Huh?"

"It was right after you told her about your Brides. Kou, I know you're aware, but I'm you, yeah?" he said, tapping the table.

With a tilt of his head, he continued seriously.

"Sometimes, there's nothing so terrifying as love."

Just then, Kou heard cheering.

There were no windows in Pandemonium's classroom, but he could still hear the sound from outside. Despite the kihei's invasion, the festival was going forward as planned.

Suddenly, a white mass came flying at him.

"Koooooooou!"

"Hey, White Princess. Don't sprint through the... Ah, she's not listening," said Kagura.

Just before the mass crashed into Kou, he expertly grabbed it in his arms. While in his embrace, the white mass rubbed its cheek against him.

In a cheery voice, the girl said, "Kou, it's the festival! It's all thanks to you! Let's go!"

"Kou...we came to meet you. We would like to see the festival with you," said Black Princess.

"Okay, I'm coming," said Kou, standing. He looked back, and Kagura waved him off.

"Have fun. You're just students right now," he said, heartfelt, if as shameless as always.

Kou hurried along, leaving Kagura behind. And all the while, he wondered:

Nothing so terrifying as love?

That was true, and Kou was painfully aware of it. After all, that was the only thing that had kept him going through hell fifteen thousand times. But what does that have to do with Asagiri?

There was something else Kou didn't understand, too.

He thought back to number five's memories.

She'd looked like a normal human girl.

A human girl who wanted to be an ally of justice.

...What are kihei...?

It was a little late to be asking that, but the question stuck with Kou. But even as he was lost in thought, his feet kept moving.

The Princesses pulled him outside.

"You finally made it. We were waiting."

"You're late, Kou. Shall we head off?"

"The stalls are the best part of the festival. Let's go conquer them all."

"Finally. We can't get started without you. Come on, let's go."

Hikami, Mirei, Tsubaki, and Yaguruma smiled at him.

Petals and light of every color bled into one another before his eyes.

The most splendid of festivals stretched out before Kou Kaguro.

The Bride of Demise

EPILOGUE

She had always thought, if there were a next time... If there were a next time. If she ever met Kou again. Maybe, just maybe, if he would let her... She would protect him, for sure this time.

Either that or she would kill him, before someone else did.

She would steal him away, before he could be stolen.

Those disturbing thoughts hadn't occurred to Asagiri right away. But ever since he'd been taken from her, right in front of her eyes, she'd been drowning in a sea of loss. And that hole that had opened up inside her had gradually reached its twisted tendrils deep into her heart. She didn't feel there was anything wrong with those thoughts.
It would be so much better than losing Kou again.
She would do anything, become anything, for Kou Kaguro.

And now a stranger was speaking to her. They were saying things. They told her it was true; Kou Kagura was alive.
Then in a smooth voice, tone soft, they asked:

"Would you like to be a Princess?"

AFTERWORD

The second volume is out. Yay!

Hello, and nice to meet you to those of you who are just joining us. This is Keishi Ayasato.

To those of you who have followed on from the first volume, thank you so much.

It makes me so happy we could meet again.

In this volume, we had a celebration in the form of a school festival.

Since this story is set in a school, I absolutely wanted to include this kind of event. I'm just glad I managed to get it done. It was really fun to write about how excited everyone was.

Of course, that wasn't all that happened. This is *The Bride of Demise*, after all.

I hope you enjoyed seeing Pandemonium having fun. I want to try writing what each person was like as the monster in the haunted house one day.

Now, on to my customary gratitude corner.

Thank you to murakaruki again for the amazing character designs and many illustrations. I am truly grateful. A huge thank you to the project managers, I and O, who I caused much grief, and to my dear family, particularly my sister. Thank you to all the designers and people involved in publishing this.

Most importantly, I would like to thank you, the readers, from the bottom of my heart.

Now, another battle is over.

Nothing would make me happier than if you continued reading.

I hope you'll continue to keep your eyes peeled for what happens to Pandemonium next.

Good-bye for now, and may we meet again.

Keishi Ayasato